Critical Acclaim For
Ross Thomas
(and Oliver Bleeck)
THE PROCANE CHRONICLE

● ● ●

"Nobody blurs the distinctions between good and evil better than Ross Thomas.... His sense of morality in an immoral age is a pillar to lean upon. And it is always so much fun to get wherever he is taking you."
— *Washington Post*

●

"The best of the American practitioners of the skulk and dagger genre ... anyone reading a Ross Thomas thriller for the first time is in imminent danger of addiction."
— *Los Angeles Times*

●

"There are very few of our contemporary entertainers as consistently entertaining as Mr. Thomas, and even fewer who can match him for style and power."
— *The New Yorker*

●

more...

ROSS THOMAS

WRITING AS OLIVER BLEECK

THE PROCANE CHRONICLE

THE MYSTERIOUS PRESS

Published by Warner Books

A Time Warner Company

MYSTERIOUS PRESS EDITION

Cover design and illustration by Peter Thorpe

This Mysterious Press Edition is published by arrangement with the author

The Mysterious Press name and logo are trademarks of Warner Books, Inc.

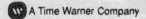 Mysterious Press Books are published by
Warner Books, Inc.
1271 Avenue of the Americas
New York, NY 10020

A Time Warner Company

Printed in the United States Of America

First Mysterious Press Printing: July, 1993
10 9 8 7 6 5 4 3 2 1

1

It was near Twenty-first Street over on Ninth Avenue, one of those decaying Chelsea blocks that look as though they've been dipped in wet soot, and except for a couple of dreary bars that kept stubborn closing hours, the laundromat was the only place open.

When it had been a pet shop a few years back the laundromat's smeared plate-glass window might have served some useful purpose—such as giving the puppies a view of the street. Now it just splashed dirty yellow light all over the sidewalk's week-long collection of garbage and trash.

At five minutes until three I drove past the laundromat in the gray Ford Galaxie that I'd rented from the Avis outlet. I drove past at six miles per hour, which was slow enough to let me count twelve flat-top washers, six tall dryers, and no customers.

Although it was cold and nearly three o'clock of a Sunday morning the small blue neon sign in the laundromat's window seemed undiscouraged as it tried to beckon some business by flashing its one-word message: Neverclose.

I drove around the block and double-parked in front of the place. I wasn't worried about a ticket. At that hour in that neighborhood I would have welcomed one along with the cop that went with it.

I got out of the car and looked around, trying to see whether there was some logical spot from where the thief might be watching. There wasn't. He could have been anyplace. Across the street in a dingy, second-floor apartment would be good. Or in a parked car. If he had field glasses, he could have been on a rooftop halfway down the block.

I made sure that I had a dime for a dryer, went back to the trunk, unlocked it, took out the blue Pan-Am carry-on bag, slung it over my left shoulder, and slammed down the lid of the trunk. I again looked around carefully, taking my time, but there was still nobody in sight. I held up my left wrist and made a show of examining my watch. It was straight up three o'clock. No one could say that I wasn't prompt.

I crossed to the plate-glass window and stared into the laundromat. The dryers were on the left; the washers were on the right. There were two backless, wooden benches near the window for customers who wanted to wait, but they were vacant except for a discarded box of Bold, an empty jug of Lysol, and a darned gray sock.

When I pushed through the glass door a dingaling bell rang, probably a holdover from the pet-shop days when there had been a proprietor on the premises. It signaled no one now. When the bell stopped ringing there was no sound at all except for a faint hum that came from the three rows of fluorescent lights.

There should have been another sound and it should have come from one of the dryers as it tumbled and tossed something that the thief had promised to wrap in a blanket. I peered through the glass of the first dryer's round door, but its gray, perforated tumbling drum was empty and still. So was the drum of the second dryer and so were they all.

The bank of six dryers protruded some three feet into the room and ended less than two feet from the rear wall, creating a shielded spot that was about half the size of a hall closet. It wasn't much space, but it was plenty of room to tuck something away out of sight, especially if it were folded just so, and that's exactly what someone had taken great pains to do.

His legs had been folded and tied so that his chin

2

rested on his knees. Ordinary brown insulation wire, the kind that is used to plug in the toaster, had been tightly knotted around his thin neck. The wire had been run beneath his bony knees so that they could be drawn up against his chest, providing a rest for his chin. The other end of the brown wire was also tied around his neck. His hands were behind him so I assumed that they, too, were tied.

I knelt down on one knee for a better look. Someone had worked him over and they had done a messy job of it. Dark bruises covered his forehead and cheeks. His nose was broken in at least one place. His lips were split and swollen. His mouth gaped open and his upper teeth were gone, although a dentist might have done that. His eyes were open, too, but nothing had been done to them. They still seemed to glisten with tears and they were still just as innocent and as blue as those of a ten-day-old kitten.

When alive those blue eyes had belonged to Bright Bobby Boykins, a dapper little man in his sixties who for more than thirty years had used their tearful innocence to work variations of the short con on the inexhaustible supply of gullible but greedy New York tourists.

I tried to remember Bobby Boykins's voice and whether it could have been the mechanically distorted one that had telephoned the instructions at 11 A.M. the previous day. If I wanted to be logical about it, that distorted telephone voice should have belonged to a thief, an expert safe man. And logically that would have eliminated Bobby Boykins because he didn't know how to peel a safe. Besides, he was too scared to have tried and too old to have learned.

I was halfway up from my kneeling position and still pondering the logic of it all when the dingaling bell sounded. I started to turn, but stopped when the voice called, "Police, fella; hold it right there!"

I held it right there, not looking left or right, not moving, trying not even to breathe. The voice sounded young and if it were young, the speaker might be inexperienced, and I wanted nothing to do with a young, inexperienced policeman.

His shoes squeaked a little as he walked toward me. "Okay," he said, "turn around toward that wall and get your hands against it. Get your feet out behind you."

I turned slowly toward the laundromat's rear wall and did just that. He was still walking toward me when he said, "Is that your gray Ford out—" He never finished the question. I thought I heard him gulp once before he whispered, "Dear sweet Jesus Christ!" which must have been how the body of Bright Bobby Boykins affected him. Or he may have said that about all dead bodies.

After a moment the young voice asked, "Is he dead?"

"He's dead."

"Did you kill him?"

"No."

"All right, fella, just hold still." He ran his hands over me quickly, not bothering to check the small of my back or the insides of my ankles. I could have been carrying a little gun or a large knife in either place, but I didn't think I should mention it. He'd learn.

"Now straighten up and put your hands behind you," the young voice said. I put my hands behind me and he snapped the handcuffs around my wrists. It was the first time that I'd ever had handcuffs on, real ones anyhow, and I didn't like the feeling. They didn't hurt, but the indignity of it all did.

"Turn around," the voice said, so I turned around and found myself facing what must have been 190 pounds or so of strapping Irish youth who wore the white crash helmet and the black-leather boots of the New York Police Department's motor-scooter patrol.

"What's your name, mister?" the young cop asked, taking out a notebook and pencil. I told him and he wrote it down after asking me how to spell it.

4

"Where d'you live?"

"The Adelphi on East Forty-sixth."

"What're you doing down here?"

"I was looking for something."

"In a laundromat? At three in the morning?" The skepticism in his tone nicely matched the incredulity on his face.

"That's right."

"What do you do? For a living, I mean."

I had to think about that one. "I'm in the mediation business." He had a little trouble spelling mediation.

"What do you mediate?"

"Disputes."

"Like labor disputes?"

"No, they're mostly private ones."

He had dark-brown eyes that took on a suspicious glow when they lit on the airline bag. "What've you got in the bag, laundry?"

I sighed. "No."

"Let's take a look."

The bag still hung by its strap over my left shoulder, but he couldn't take it off because of the way he had handcuffed me. He fiddled with it a moment and then told me to turn around. He unlocked the left cuff, removed the bag, and snapped the cuff back on. I turned back around and watched him carry the bag over to the top of a washer. He slid the zipper back and looked inside. His face told me that he had never seen ninety thousand dollars before. Not in cash. Few people have.

First he blushed and then he said, "Goddamn." He said it reverently. He was going to say something else, but the dingaling bell jangled as the door burst open and two men streaked in, a little crouched over, their topcoats open and flapping, and their snub-nosed revolvers aimed right at me.

One of them was blond and the other one was bald and neither was much past thirty. The blond one said, "What's going on here?" Although he looked at me he

5

was talking to the young uniformed policeman who had spun around at the sound of the dingaling bell, clawing at his still holstered revolver. He had quit clawing when he saw the two men.

"I was just gonna call it in," the young uniformed policeman said, apparently recognizing the two men.

"You were gonna call what in?" the blond man said, still pointing his revolver at me.

The young officer waved in my direction. "This one was messing around in here when I came by so I stopped and came in and caught him bending over a dead one and then I looked in his bag here and he's got a whole pisspot full of money."

The blond man held open his coat and put the revolver back in the holster that he wore on the left side of his belt. The bald man put his gun away too.

"You say there's a dead one?" the blond man said.

"Yes, sir."

"You know how to call a dead one in?"

"Yes, sir."

"Then do it."

The young policeman nodded and hurried for the door. The blond man waited until the dingaling bell quit ringing and then said to me, "We'll get around to you in a minute. My name's Deal. Detective Deal. That's Detective Oller. We're Homicide South. That hold you?"

I nodded. "That'll hold me."

Deal said, "Take a look in the bag, Ollie," and then moved past me toward the corner that concealed the body of Bobby Boykins. I moved back and watched as he stared at the body for several seconds. He squatted down for a better look and then used his right hand to touch Boykins's forehead, as if trying to determine whether the dead man was running a fever. Still gazing at the body, Deal called, "What's in the bag, Ollie?"

"Just like the kid said. Money. A whole pisspot full."

Deal rose and turned. "How much?"

"I haven't counted it, but it looks like it's over fifty thousand," Oller said. "Way over."

"Count it," Deal said, turning his stare on me again.

"There's ninety thousand in the bag," I said.

Deal's stare came from a pair of gray eyes that had the color and warmth of old slush. He was a little taller than I, slightly over six feet, lean, and vain enough to use something on his shock of straw-colored hair to keep it brushed just so. Probably hair spray. His face was beginning to grow some lines and none of them turned up. He had no visible scars on his face, but with that slash of a mouth, he wouldn't need any.

He kept on staring at me until Oller finished counting and announced, "It's like he said, ninety thousand."

"Take a look in the corner," Deal said. "See if you know him."

Oller left the airline bag on the washer, went behind me, and said, "They tied him up good, didn't they? Like a Christmas turkey."

"You know him?" Deal said.

"Never saw him before," Oller said and came over to help inspect me. Oller was heavier than Deal by about twenty pounds and a good bit of it was fat. The fat somehow went with his bald head. He also had a nice start on a double chin and what little hair he had left was flecked with gray. His bright black eyes danced around a lot underneath heavy brows. His nose turned up, but he kept the ends of a wide, moist mouth turned down. It was still a young face, but the kind that can turn old in a week.

"Who's he?" Oller said, nodding at me.

"I don't know," Deal said. "Maybe he's just a guy who turns on by hanging around dead bodies in laun-

7

dromats at three in the morning. Maybe the ninety thousand bucks helps."

"Okay, mister," Oller said, "what's your name?"

"Philip St. Ives."

"Where do you live?"

"The Adelphi on East Forty-sixth."

"You know the dead guy?"

"I knew him. Not well."

"What's his name?"

"Bobby Boykins."

"What'd he do?"

"I think he was retired."

"What'd he do before he retired?"

"I think he was a con man."

"What do you do?"

"I'm sort of retired, too."

"You mean you were sort of planning to retire on that ninety thousand bucks?" Deal said.

"No."

"Does it belong to you?"

"No."

"Who does it belong to?"

"A friend."

"What's your friend's name?"

I shook my head. "I don't think I'd better say anything else until I talk to a lawyer."

Deal nodded, almost indifferently, I thought. "Read him about his rights, Ollie." Oller fished out a small card and in a bored voice read what the Supreme Court had ruled that they were supposed to read to me. It had a somehow comforting sound.

"You're under arrest, Mr. St. Ives," Deal said.

"For what?"

"Suspicion of murder and grand larceny."

"All right."

"It doesn't seem to worry you much," Oller said.

"It worries me."

"It would worry the shit out of me," Oller said.

"This the first time you ever been arrested?" Deal said.

"Yes."

"I don't think you're going to like it."

"I don't think so either," I said.

2

The three of them finally took me in, Deal, Oller, and the young patrolman whose name turned out to be Francis X. Frann. They let him be the arresting officer, perhaps because a murder one might look good on his record.

We didn't have far to drive, just over to the Tenth Precinct on West Twentieth. We went past the desk officer, a middle-aged sergeant who looked at me without any curiosity at all, and then Deal and Oller took me up one flight to the detective squad room where somebody else took my fingerprints.

"You can make three phone calls," Deal said, handing me a jar of jellied cleanser and some paper towels to get the ink off my fingers.

"I thought it was just one," I said.

"Three," he said. "If they're local."

"I want to call Connecticut," I said. "Darien."

"That's long distance," Deal said.

"I'll pay for it."

"Who do you want to call?" Deal said.

"Myron Greene. There's an *e* on the end of Greene."

Deal asked me whether I had the number, wrote it

down when I told him what it was, and then said, "What's Greene, your lawyer?"

"He's a little more than that," I said.

"What?"

"He's the guy who got me into this mess."

It had begun late Friday morning when the pumpkin arrived a quarter of an hour before Myron Greene did. I had already carved the top off the pumpkin and was sending the seeds and the fiber down the disposal when I heard his knock. I turned off the disposal and carried the pumpkin over to the hexagonal poker table that I'd covered with the October twenty-ninth edition of the *Times*. After letting Myron Greene in I asked, "What do you know about jack-o'-lanterns?"

"Everything," he said and moved over to the poker table to give the pumpkin what he must have felt was an expert appraisal.

"Well?" I said.

"God knows, it's big enough."

"The bell captain got it for me."

"Eddie?"

"Eddie."

Myron Greene used the stem to lift off the top. He peered inside. "You did a good job of cleaning it out. How much did it cost?"

"Ten bucks."

He shook his head a little sadly, much as he would have done were I to tell him that I'd decided to take a flyer on pork-belly futures. "When's the last time you bought a pumpkin?"

"It's been a while," I said.

"That's a three-dollar pumpkin. Maybe three-fifty. I could have got you one in Darien for two."

"As big?"

"Almost."

"Well, Eddie had to take a cab."

"To the pumpkin farm?"

"I didn't ask."

Myron Greene shook his head again as he shrugged out of his topcoat whose brown-and-cream checks were patterned after a hound's tooth, the Hound of the Baskervilles probably. He glanced around as if searching for some place to hang the coat or for me to remember my manners. I reached for it and saw that it could also be worn as a cape. I'd always thought of Myron Greene as one of those persons who manages to stay just behind the latest fashion and that topcoat and double-breasted brown suit and his fat, old gold tie did nothing to change my opinion.

He pulled a chair out from the table, made sure that its seat was clean, and settled into it with the air of a man who wants to talk about something that may take a while. "Draw it first," he said.

"The face?"

"A soft lead pencil's good."

I found an Edo King 503, the last of what must have been a gross or two of pencils that I'd brought home one by one, or two by two, from a long defunct and little mourned newspaper that I'd once worked for, and started to sketch a jack-o'-lantern's face on the pumpkin's flame-colored skin.

"Make the eyes slanted," Greene said. "You don't want a happy-looking jack-o'-lantern."

I made the eyes slanted and then turned the pumpkin all the way around for his inspection. He nodded. "Sinister," he said. "That's how they like them to look. Sinister."

"He's only six."

"At six they really like them sinister. When did you last see him, Saturday?"

I nodded. "This'll be his first jack-o'-lantern."

"How does he like his new stepfather?"

"Fine," I said. "When he grows older and realizes how rich his stepfather is, he'll like him even better." I rose, moved over to the Pullman kitchen, found the paring knife, and came back to the table. The knife sank easily into the pumpkin. I cut out a triangle for

11

the nose and again turned the pumpkin for Myron Greene's inspection. He nodded and I turned it back and started to work on the eyes. They were harder to do than the nose.

"Who do we talk about that you couldn't talk about over the phone?" I said.

"I didn't say we couldn't; I said I didn't want to."

"How rich is he?"

"What makes you think he's rich?"

"Because you said he was a client and you don't have any other kind. Except me."

"You're not exactly starving now that she's remarried and you're off the alimony hook."

"I haven't worked in a while."

"Nine months," Myron Greene said. "You haven't worked in nine months."

"That's a while."

"You've had some opportunities," he said.

"I wouldn't call them that."

"That oil company was a most reputable firm," Myron Greene said as he rose and moved around the table so that he could see how I was coming with the teeth. The teeth were even harder to do than the eyes.

"I don't know of many reputable oil firms who go around ransoming kidnapped South American generals," I said.

Greene went back to his seat on the other side of the table. "I'm still convinced that the kidnappers would have returned the general, if they'd been paid."

I looked up at him and shook my head. "And I'm convinced that the go-between the oil company finally hired was smart to skip with the money. If he hadn't, the kidnappers would have killed him, just like they killed the general."

"Well, this isn't anything like that."

"It'd better not be."

"It seems a simple enough transaction."

"As long as it has nothing to do with the diplomatic

12

set," I said. "I don't know why, Myron, but a call from the State Department can somehow convince you that the Republic will founder unless I'm on the next plane to Belgrade. Well, I tried that once and you know what happened."

Myron Greene sniffed, as if he remembered something that smelled bad. "It happened nearer to Sarajevo," he said, "and the entire scheme was incredibly inept—which I pointed out to the Secretary in my letter, if you remember."

"I remember his reply better," I said. "He said he'd never heard of me."

By now I had been Myron Greene's client for nearly six years. Before that I had written a newspaper column that dealt mostly with the life styles of those New Yorkers who made their livings by doing something or other that the law said they shouldn't. Most of the people I had written about were small time grifters, con men, hustlers, assorted thieves, and unlucky horse players.

One of my constant readers had been an occasional thief who had once stolen some jewelry from one of Myron Greene's clients and then had offered to sell it all back providing that I served as the go-between. Greene had approached me and I had agreed. Shortly after I had bought the jewelry back the paper folded and I was among the unemployed until Greene again approached me, this time to serve as the go-between in a kidnapping.

Because there seemed to be a better than fair chance that I might get shot or dumped in the East River, I was paid ten thousand dollars for my efforts, which was ten percent of the ransom figure, and quite a bit more than anyone really believed my life to be worth.

After that, I became Myron Greene's client—or he became my keeper. He paid my bills, handled my income tax, reluctantly saw me through my divorce, and collected ten percent of whatever I earned in a calling

13

that wasn't terribly overcrowded and which offered a service that promised to remain in demand as long as thieves stole things from people, or, in some instances, stole people from people.

I think Myron Greene kept me on as a client not because he needed the money, but because he felt that anyone who rubbed shoulders with thieves must dwell far beyond the pale of respectability in a land peopled by marvelously free souls who lived swift-moving lives, never grew old, and got up late in the morning. He seemed to find it all rather dashing and because I treasured my own illusions, I saw no reason to destroy his.

Through Myron Greene the go-between assignments came my way two or three or even four times a year. They paid the rent on my ninth-floor "deluxe" efficiency in the Adelphi on East Forty-sixth, allowed me to patronize, if not frequent, a few of the better saloons, let me travel whenever the mood struck, which it did less and less, and enabled me to ignore the help wanted ads, except for a sneak glance or two on Sunday.

So now there was the possibility of another assignment and after I finished the jack-o'-lantern's mouth, I turned the pumpkin around for Greene's inspection. "Tell me about your client," I said.

Greene tilted his head to one side as if trying to make up his mind about whether the jack-o'-lantern was an example of true folk art. "He's a man of moderate means and—"

"What's moderate?"

He looked up at the ceiling and gave his $12.50 haircut a thoughtful pat. "He has some rather nice holdings, but nothing spectacular. He's worth around two million, I'd say. Possibly three."

"Manages to scrape by."

"All right, damn it, he's not poor. If it weren't for the wealthy, you'd have to find a job."

"You're wrong, Myron. If it weren't for the thieves, I'd have to find a job."

Myron Greene reached for the paring knife, pulled the pumpkin over, and started doing something to its mouth. "Let's agree that my client is of moderately substantial means. Does that satisfy you?"

"Perfectly."

He turned the pumpkin around. I don't know what he had done to the mouth, but it looked far more sinister.

"How's that?" he said.

"Much better."

Greene leaned back so that he could admire his handiwork. "My new client was recommended to me by his broker, an old friend of mine, who asked me to take him on as a personal favor. That was a little over three weeks ago and I really haven't done much for the client—just some routine work. He called late yesterday and wanted to know if you were available. I told him I'd find out."

"You want a drink?" I said.

Myron Greene looked at his watch. "It's a little early, isn't it?"

"Probably."

"Well—"

"I'll make it weak." I went over to the sink and mixed Greene's drink and one for myself so he wouldn't feel that he was sinning alone. "What's he want?" I said.

"I'm getting to that."

"Here," I said, handing him his drink.

He tasted it suspiciously. "Well, while my client was away over the weekend, someone broke into his house and stole certain personal documents. Two days ago whoever stole the documents called him and offered to sell them back for a substantial sum."

"How much?"

"One hundred thousand."

"What kind of personal documents?"

15

"My client would prefer not to say."

"Come on, Myron, I can't handle it unless I know what I'm buying."

"Well, I can say that the documents are in the form of a diary that goes back twenty-five years."

"Nobody keeps a diary that long unless he's never grown up."

Myron Greene stiffened his face. "My client is just past fifty."

I decided to light a cigarette, my first in over an hour. By tapping some heretofore unsuspected reserves of self-discipline, I had cut down to a pack and a half a day. I kidded myself that I would stop altogether by Christmas. Or maybe New Year's.

"They must be incriminating," I said. "If they weren't, nobody would steal them. And he'd never spend that much just to check back on whether it was the winter of fifty or fifty-one that he caught the tarpon off Bermuda."

Myron Greene frowned and the resulting wrinkles were thoughtfully legal and made him look wise and grave beyond his thirty-six years. It was a look that would have gone over well with a jury, but Myron Greene was far too good a lawyer to ever let a case of his be decided by twelve strangers. When he spoke, his tone was as grave as his look.

"A person," he said, "can place a high premium on the privacy of his past without it meaning that his past necessarily entails something incriminating." He paused to frown some more. "Privacy commands its own price, especially if one is a person of means."

I thought some of that was arguable, but I shrugged and said, "All right, who suggested me?"

"The thief. Or thieves."

"And your client agrees?"

"That's why he called me."

"What do you think?"

Myron Greene decided to examine the ceiling again. "It seems straightforward enough," he said.

"And you can certainly use the ten thousand. Incidentally, it'll come off the top of the hundred thousand. The thief stipulated that when he asked for you."

"That's unusual," I said.

"Yes. That's what I thought."

"All right," I said after a moment. "I'll take it. What's your client's name?"

"Abner Procane."

I was trying to swallow some of my drink when Myron Greene said the name and the drink stopped about halfway down and then backed up, a lot of it spurting out of my nose. After I got through coughing and blowing Myron Greene said, "What was all that supposed to mean?"

"It means," I said, "that your new client is probably the best thief in town."

3

Detective Deal had used the area code to direct-dial the Darien number and the phone rang nine times before Myron Greene's voice came on, sleepy and thick, with a muttered, "Hello."

"This is St. Ives," I said. "I'm in jail."

"Ah, Jesus. It's almost four."

"If you don't wake up, it's going to be five and I'll still be in jail."

There was a pause and then Greene said, "All right, I'm awake," and his voice sounded crisp and alert. Maybe his wife had brought him a cold cloth. "Where are you?"

"The Tenth Precinct on West Twentieth."

"'What's the charge?'"

"They're thinking about two of them. Suspicion of murder one and grand larceny."

"Jesus," Myron Greene said again and then asked, "What happened?" I told him what I could, making it as succinct as possible. There was a brief silence while he probably sorted through his bag of legal tricks. "What have you told them?" he finally asked.

"My name and address."

"All right," he said. "I'm going to have to call some people and it's going to take a while. I'll try to keep our client's name out of it and that may be difficult and time-consuming, so you'd better plan on spending a little more time right where you are. But I'll try to get you out before they send the wagon around in the morning to take you downtown."

"I don't like it here," I said, "but I'd like it even less in the Tombs."

"I'll get back to you."

"Do that," I said and hung up.

"You want to call anybody else?" Deal said.

I shook my head. "No."

"Then let's go down and talk to Sergeant Finn."

Sergeant Finn, the desk officer, still looked bored, even when they told him about the dead body of Bobby Boykins. He perked up a little though when they got around to the ninety thousand dollars and agreed that it wouldn't do at all to turn me loose upon society and that they should hang on to me for a few more hours. By then they would have talked to someone in the district attorney's office and the wagon would be around to haul me down to the Complaint Court at 100 Centre Street.

After that they made me empty my pockets and an elderly cop sniffed as if to see whether I'd been drinking, apparently decided that I hadn't, and let me keep my cigarettes and matches. Then they took me back upstairs to the detective squad room.

It was a medium-sized room, about fifteen by

twenty, with four gray metal desks, a couple of type-writers, and a tacky-looking bulletin board with a reward poster on it offering $5,000 for the arrest and conviction of somebody who'd stolen $600,000. The walls were two shades of green—medium dark to about halfway up and then light green all the way to the white ceiling. The floor was covered with black asphalt tile and didn't show the dirt much.

Just off the squad room was another, smaller room with two desks, four chairs, and brown walls. They put me in there, closed the door, and forgot about me.

I sat down in one of the chairs and felt sorry for myself, the way the falsely accused always do. The precinct didn't have any cells, just a detention cage for the violent cases that was made out of green iron mesh, and I told myself that I was lucky they hadn't put me in there because it contained nothing to sit on other than the floor.

I had a fairly nice time feeling sorry for myself, smoking cigarettes, and wondering about how frightened I might become. When I got tired of that, I thought about Abner Procane, the thief who kept diaries.

Not too many persons in New York suspected that Abner Procane was a thief. A few cops did, but they had never been able to prove it and after a while they didn't even bother to try. Some of the racier types that I occasionally palled around with assumed that Procane was a thief, but because they couldn't figure a percentage for themselves, they weren't really interested.

When I had got through telling Myron Greene on that pre-Halloween Friday about what I suspected Procane to be, Greene had replied, "Hearsay. That's all you have. Pure hearsay."

"That's sometimes all you need when you're a reporter."

"Well, you're not a reporter now."

"I was when I first heard about him."

"Ah, but you didn't write it, did you?"

I had let that pass and said, "What if he is a thief, would you still be his lawyer?"

"I've seen his holdings; the man couldn't possibly be a thief."

"But if he were?"

The idea of being a top thief's counsel had delighted Myron Greene, of course. But he wouldn't admit it. Instead, he had drawn himself up a little stiffly and said, "Every man is entitled to representation. Of course, I'd be his lawyer."

"All right then, I'll be his go-between."

I'd first heard about Abner Procane some six or seven years back when Billie Fowler came out of retirement to try his skill on a new Mosler 125-S executive wall safe that was supposed to contain twenty-five thousand or so that an eye, ear, nose, and throat doctor had forgotten to report to the Internal Revenue Service.

Billie had opened the safe without too much trouble and was cleaning it out when he was hit by a heart attack. The doctor discovered him the next morning, still sprawled in front of the half-empty safe, his pockets stuffed with fifty-dollar bills. They had made a deal. The doctor agreed to get Billie to a hospital if Billie agreed not to tell the IRS about the twenty-five thousand dollars.

It was another one of those stories that I couldn't write and Billie, sensing my disappointment, had tugged at his hospital gown, and said, "Why don't you do a write-up on Abner Procane?"

"Who's he?"

"You never heard it from me, unnerstand?"

"All right. Who is he?"

"He's the best thief in town, that's who. Maybe the best thief in the whole fuckin world. You wanna know why?"

"Why?"

"Because he never steals nothing but money. But you never got it from me, right?"

"Right."

I started to poke around a little and the next word I got on Procane came from an old-time con man who liked to boast that he'd helped take J. Frank Norfleet for forty-five thousand dollars in the famous Denver big store back during the twenties. He claimed to have heard that Procane had stolen more than five million dollars in his time. "Now that's a hell of a lot of money," the old man had said and after a couple of more drinks, we'd both agreed that it was probably too much.

I had some vague idea of doing a column on Procane so I kept checking on him in a haphazard fashion. One fairly successful ex-thief who had turned Jehovah's Witness claimed that he had heard of the poor sinner and even prayed for him whenever he thought about it, which wasn't often.

"But I don't think it does any good," he'd added, as we stood there on the corner at Forty-third and Broadway. "The guy's never taken a fall and I hear that he don't pull but one job every year or so. Now what kind of a thief is that?" A smart one, we'd both agreed. "I don't even know what jobs he was supposed to have been in on," the reformed thief had said as he stuck a copy of *The Watchtower* under the nose of a passing cop.

If the rumors that I heard about Procane were spicy, the facts that I dug up were dull. He had been born to middle-class New Canaan, Connecticut, parents in 1920 and after a totally uneventful childhood and adolescence, had been graduated from Cornell with an engineering degree in 1941. The army had sent him overseas in 1943 as a second lieutenant. He took his discharge in Marseilles in 1945 and remained there until late 1946 when he returned to New York and married Wilmetta Foulkes who died in an airline crash five years later. There were no children and the story about the plane crash was the only time Procane's name had even appeared in a New York paper.

He had never been arrested. He had never been employed. He lived in a town house on East Seventy-fourth and employed a Negro housekeeper who arrived at 10 A.M. and left at 7 P.M., Monday through Friday. Procane spent most of his weekends at a run-down farm that he owned in Connecticut. His phone number in New York was unlisted. The Connecticut farm had no phone.

I'd kept on checking him out in my own desultory fashion, not pressing too hard because I really wasn't much of a muckraker, preferring instead to write about the human foibles of our time, probably because I could so easily identify with nearly all of them.

One afternoon, almost six months after I had first heard about Procane, I found myself drinking draft beer in an East Orange, New Jersey, bar with a retired Manhattan detective sergeant and the chief investigator of one of the larger casualty insurance companies. Because we were running out of things to lie about, I brought up the name of Abner Procane.

"I hear he's a thief," I said, again demonstrating my faith in the disarming effect of the subtle query.

"You hear from who?" said the detective sergeant who for reasons known only to himself and God had selected East Orange as his retirement haven. His name was Seymour Rhynes.

"Other thieves," I said.

"They don't know nothing," Rhynes said. "I bet they can't even name you one job he's pulled."

"I can," the insurance investigator said. He was a mild-looking South Carolinian who wore rimless glasses, clip-on bow ties, and favored shapeless gray worsted suits, winter and summer. His name was Howard Calloway.

Rhynes let his suspicious blue eyes wander over

22

Calloway. After a while he nodded and said, "Yeah, maybe you can."

"What was it?" I said.

"About five years ago there was this United States senator that we had a floater policy on," Calloway said. "Well, it seems that the senator had come into a hundred thousand in cash. He kept it locked away in a suitcase in his suite in the Shoreham down in Washington. Well, one day Procane knocks at his door, sticks a gun in his stomach, handcuffs him to the radiator, gags him, goes right to the closet, takes out the suitcase that holds the hundred grand, nods good-bye, and leaves.

"Well, a maid discovers the senator and when the cops come, he tells them that he has to make an important phone call. So he calls us and wants to know if his floater policy will cover a hundred thousand in cash. So we ask if he's reported it and he says no, not yet. Then he hems and haws a little and says maybe it wasn't a hundred thousand after all. He finally tells the cops that he only got hurt for two hundred dollars."

"How'd you know it was Procane?" I said.

Calloway shrugged. "Luck mostly. One of our men was going back up to New York from Washington and spotted Procane on the shuttle. He kept an eye on him till he caught a cab and he was carrying a fancy bag just like the senator put in a claim for."

"Where'd the hundred thousand come from?" I said, not really expecting an answer.

Calloway looked into his beer. "I don't think that's as interesting as trying to figure out how Procane knew it was in the closet. We settled the senator's claim for the two hundred cash he lost plus another two hundred bucks for the bag."

"What'd you do about Procane?"

"Nothing," Rhynes said. "What could we do?"

"Could the senator identify him?"

"Sure," Calloway said. "But he wouldn't, because if Procane knew that the hundred thousand dollars was in the closet, he also knew where it came from, and the senator wasn't about to bring that out in the open."

Rhynes picked up the pitcher of beer and filled all three glasses. "They say he knocked over a high-stakes poker game at the Waldorf in fifty-nine for close to seventy-five thousand. They say that in 1964 he took close to a hundred thousand out of the wall safe of a Park Avenue shrink. They say that last fall he stopped more than seventy grand in juice money that was supposed to be on its way to a city councilman. It never got there. They say."

"I heard about the juice money," Calloway said. "I never heard about the others."

"Well, we sure as hell never heard about them officially. I never heard about the senator before either."

"No complaints, huh?" I said to Rhynes.

He shook his big head that was shaped like a wrinkled bullet and said, "Who's to complain? The city councilman? The shrink who's cheating the government? The big-shot muckety-mucks who're playing high-stakes poker, and one of them the head of a big charity outfit?"

"How do you know it was Procane?" I said.

"What would you say to an eyewitness?" Rhynes said.

"That would be pretty good."

"Well, this bagman who was carrying the seventy big ones got a little upset, know what I mean?"

"I think so," I said.

"He didn't think the guy who'd given him the money to deliver would be too understanding, so he comes to us and asks for protection. Well, what could we do? There wasn't no evidence, just his story. So we showed him some pictures of Procane that we'd taken with a long-distance lens and he says, 'That's the son

24

of a bitch, all right.' But still, what could we do? If we talked to Procane, all he'd have to do is laugh and say, 'What seventy thousand?' And the guy who was gonna juice the councilman with it sure as hell wasn't about to admit anything. So all we had was the bagman's story, which wasn't worth nothing, so we finally turned him loose."

"What happened to him?" I said.

Rhynes took a deep draught of beer and then said, "He sort of went away."

"I reckon that fella Procane's my favorite thief," Calloway said. "One, he never steals anything but money. Two, he never steals it from anyone who'll make a complaint about it. And three, I'm not so sure he'll ever get caught."

Rhynes belched. It was a rumbling one that started as a harsh crackle and ended as a mild roar. "Oh, he'll get caught one of these days," he said, patting his belly comfortably. There was plenty to pat.

"When?" I said.

"When he finally gets careless," he said, nodding his head with the absolute certainty that's born of thirty years' experience. "They finally all get careless, you know."

"Bullshit," Calloway said as politely as it can be said. "I don't agree with that at all. Not at all. Procane might get himself caught one day, but it won't be by the cops."

"Who by?" I said.

"If he doesn't get himself killed by someone he's stealing from, he'll get hurt in a different way and it'll hurt bad. Real bad."

"How?"

"Someday," Calloway said in a voice made thoughtful by five beers, "somebody's gonna steal something from Mr. Abner Procane because he's gone and made himself such a big, fat target. And when that day comes I'd like to be around just so I could watch Procane."

"Watch him do what?" I said.

"I don't know," Calloway said. "That's why I'd wanta watch."

4

They came for me at six o'clock and took me back downstairs without saying a word. They took me into a small room that I hadn't been in before and a young, uniformed policeman handed me back the contents of my pockets.

"What now?" I said.

"Wait here," he said and shoved a form at me. "Count your money, check your possessions, and sign this. It's our receipt."

I counted the money in my billfold and signed the receipt. "Is it all there?" the young cop said, not because he cared, but because it was what they had told him to say.

"I'm short about ninety thousand."

"You break me up," he said, turned and left.

It was another grim, bare room that contained nothing but a gray table and two matching chairs. I sat down in one of them and waited some more. In about fifteen minutes the door opened and Detectives Deal and Oller came in. Deal carried the blue airline bag. Neither of them looked as if they had had any sleep.

"You got nice connections, St. Ives," Deal said,

placing the bag on the table. "Real nice. They're going to let you walk."

"When?"

"When you finish counting the money," Oller said and unzipped the bag. "You can start any time."

I started counting and they watched. When I was nearly a fourth of the way through, Deal said, "That money kept the kid up all night, you know."

"What kid?" I said, almost losing my count.

"Officer Frann. You remember Officer Frann. He put the cuffs on you."

I nodded and kept on counting.

"He stayed up all night making a record of all the serial numbers on the money," Deal said. "That was before anybody told us what you did for a living. You got quite a reputation downtown, you know."

"I didn't," I said, dropped a thousand in my count, and went back to pick it up.

"Of course, me and Deal being in homicide, we wouldn't have much call to do any business with you, unless somebody wanted to ransom a dead body, and we haven't run across one like that yet."

"Yet," Deal said and then they were both silent until I finished the count and zipped up the bag.

"It's all there," I said, and signed another form that Oller handed me.

"If you go ahead and turn that money over to whoever you were planning to turn it over to, are you going to tell em that we got the serial numbers?" Deal said. "That's strictly an unofficial question. I just got curious."

"No," I said. "I'll get them a new batch."

"You sort of like to cooperate with thieves, huh?" Oller said.

"I sometimes have to," I said.

Deal nodded as if trying to show that he found that perfectly understandable. He almost succeeded. "Well, you're no longer a suspect now that we got it on the very best downtown authority that you're not the type who'd go around killing anybody like that old guy we found trussed up in the laundromat. But me and Oller were sort of wondering if we might drop by and ask you a few questions? As a witness, I mean, not as a suspect."

"Any time," I said and waited for the rest of it, the part that wouldn't be quite so polite.

"We might drop around more than once," Oller said and gave me a bleak smile that somehow failed to go with his fat man's face.

"And you might even drop around to see us," Deal said and they cracked out the rest of it: "Like tomorrow at ten A.M."

"You want a statement," I said, seeing no reason to make it a question.

"That's right," Oller said.

"Where?"

"You know where Homicide South is?"

"Yes."

"Just ask for either of us."

"Oller and Deal."

"Carl Oller," Deal said, "and Frank Deal."

"Can I go now?"

"Sure," Deal said, "if you don't mind answering just one little personal question?"

"What?"

"Doesn't this business you're in sort of make you a little sick when you look in the mirror?"

"Sure," I said, "but I usually take something for it."

"What?"

"Money."

Myron Greene was waiting for me at the entrance to the Tenth Precinct and we went down the two steps and made our way through the small knot of uniformed cops who were admiring Greene's new and unticketed de Tomaso Mangusta that he had just traded his Shelby Cobra for. Before that, he had owned an Excalibur until someone had told him it was corny.

We didn't speak until we had fitted ourselves inside the thing and Myron had revved it up a couple of times to the cops' delight. Then we streaked off down Twentieth Street for about fifty yards to where the red light was.

"Who'd you have to call?" I said.

"An assistant district attorney and a guy in the mayor's office that I went to school with."

Sometimes I felt that Myron Greene had gone to school with half of the nation's public servants. The other half had gone to Yale.

"Anyone else?"

He turned to look at me. "Procane."

"What did he say?"

"He was concerned, of course."

"So am I."

"He wants to see you."

"When?"

"Now, if you can make it."

"I'm pretty scruffy."

"He thinks it's quite important, and I agree with him."

"Why?" I said and grabbed for something to hold on to as Greene drifted his eleven-thousand-dollar machine around the corner and up Sixth Avenue.

"Because," he said, "he got a call this morning from somebody else who wants to sell him back his diaries."

I had met Abner Procane for the first time only the day before, but it now seemed weeks ago. Yesterday had been October thirtieth, a Saturday, and there had been just enough bite in the air to make the long walk from Forty-sixth to Seventy-fourth a pleasure instead of an ordeal. I like to walk in New York on Saturday mornings when the weather is fine and the people are few—or relatively so. It reminds me of what the city

29

was like twenty years ago when I first saw it as a visiting teen-ager from Ohio. It had held a lot more promise then. But so had I.

As New York neighborhoods go, Procane's was fairly clean. At least I didn't have to wade through the garbage because most of it was neatly tied up in green plastic bags. The bags seem like a good idea to me, but I'm sure there must be something wrong with them, just as there's something wrong with disposable bottles and flip-top beer cans. It may be that children can crawl into the bags and suffocate. I don't know that this is true, but it's something else to worry about.

Myron Greene had set our appointment for ten o'clock and at one minute past ten I was scraping dog shit off my left shoe on the bottom step of Procane's four-story town house. He must have been waiting for me because he came out to watch.

"I could never understand those who keep large dogs in a city such as this," he said, much as he might have mentioned it to a neighbor who lived four doors down.

"I'm a cat man myself," I said. "They like to crap in private."

After I cleaned off my shoe I went up the steps and shook hands with him. He had a firm, dry shake, much like what you would expect from a CPA or a high school principal.

"You're a bit younger than I thought you'd be," he said, and to prove it he let his face display some mild surprise. But then he had a mild face, almost round, with thinning hair the color of old ginger, greenish eyes widely spaced above a broad nose, a moustache of sorts that had more gray in it than did his hair, a pleasant enough mouth that seemed to move around a lot, even in repose, and a round chin that went nicely with everything else.

He opened a wrought-iron gate that barred the way to his front door, which he unlocked with a key, and then we were in a thoughtfully furnished hallway.

Procane crossed to a door and held it open. "I think this will be comfortable," he said.

I entered a rather large room that seemed to be half office and half study. Its windows fronted on Seventy-fourth. There was a fireplace, which was working, a carved desk, a lot of books, some chairs, a leather couch raised at one end like the psychiatrists in cartoons have and which I've been unable to find, a large globe, and a number of oil paintings of some pleasant rural scenes.

Procane walked over to an electric coffee pot and filled two waiting cups. "Cream and sugar?" he said.

"A little sugar."

"Do sit down," he said and after I chose a comfortable-looking chair next to the fire he handed me a cup. He lowered himself into a chair opposite mine and, what with the fire going, I thought it to be all rather cheery.

"I assume that Mr. Greene filled most of it in for you," Procane said.

"He told me what he knew," I said, "but he didn't mention one thing because he didn't know it."

"What was that?"

"That you're supposed to be the best thief in town."

I'm still not quite sure what response I expected from Procane. Perhaps nothing more than the cool smile I got.

"You did some checking on me about six or seven years ago when you were still with the paper, didn't you?"

"Yes."

"I was pleased, but surprised that you never wrote anything."

"I could never find a fact to hang it on."

"Would a fact or two now help things along?"

"It might."

Procane shifted his gaze from me to the fire. Then he smiled slightly and said, "You're quite right, Mr. St. Ives; I am a thief."

31

5

According to Abner Procane, he never stole anything in his life until he was twenty-five years old. He was in the army then and he stole a truckload of American cigarettes and sold them on the Marseilles black market. He sold them to a man called Marcel Comegys, and if it hadn't been for Comegys, Procane would be in jail today. At least that's what Procane thought.

"He was a master thief and he taught me how to steal, what to steal, and whom to steal it from," Procane said.

Comegys taught Procane to steal only money and to steal it only from those who were in no position to complain about their losses to the police.

"That may be the reason that I've never had any professional dealings with you before, Mr. St. Ives," he said. "One doesn't ransom money."

The rest of what Procane told me rounded out the story that I had already put together. He stole but once or twice a year, and then only after the most meticulous planning. He had a high overhead, because he had to pay and pay well for information about his potential victims. And, not surprisingly, he enjoyed his work.

"I like to steal," Procane said as he rose, picked up a brass poker, and stirred up the logs in the fireplace. "It's not a compulsion, but from the first there was something about theft that intrigued and excited me. I don't think there's anything sexual about it either— not much, at any rate. The nearest thing that I can

32

compare it to is painting, if there were more action in painting. Stealing gives me the same sense of—well, of achievement, except that it's much more intensified."

"You seem to have thought about it a lot," I said.

"Too much probably." He turned to look at a painting of a much weathered barn that was shaded by trees.

"Yours?" I said.

He nodded. I looked at the painting more carefully. The trees were beeches, I decided. It was a summer scene and I thought he had caught the sunlight rather well.

"Those diaries of yours must be hot stuff," I said.

"They are more of a journal than a diary," Procane said. "When I hear the word diary I always think of the wistful hopes of terribly inexperienced young girls. After a little experience, they stop keeping them."

"What did you keep your journal in?" I said.

"You mean what do they look like?"

"Yes."

"In ordinary one-hundred-page ledgers, approximately eight and a half by fourteen inches. They're black with fake red-leather triangles to protect the right-hand corners. You can buy them at any office-supply store. I did."

"How many of them are there?"

"Five, and they cover twenty-five years."

"How'd it happen?"

Procane smiled a little. "I suppose it's a little like the cobbler whose children have no shoes. I have this small farm in Connecticut." He gestured toward the paintings. "They were all done there. I was at the farm last weekend and when I returned I discovered I'd been burglarized. By an expert."

"Where did you keep them?"

"In an old safe that came with the house. I've been intending to replace it for years, but—" He shrugged.

"Was it punched, peeled or what?" I said.

"Peeled."

"How'd they get in?"

"Through the front door. They walked in."

"Your locks look pretty good."

"They didn't bother the thief. Or thieves. Neither did my burglar-alarm systems, which are supposed to be the best."

"When did they call you? I don't know why I keep saying 'they.'"

"I do it, too," Procane said. "A man called Wednesday morning and told me he wanted a hundred thousand dollars to return the journals. Then he said that he wanted you to handle the payment and that your services would cost me nothing, because you could take your ten percent off the top. I was surprised when he told me that Myron Greene was your attorney because I had just retained Greene. It was something of a coincidence and I'm not too fond of coincidences."

"Neither am I," I said and we looked at each other for a while as if trying to think of something suspicious to say. When we couldn't, I said, "What did the thief say he'd do, if you didn't pay up?"

"He'd send them to the police."

"And you wouldn't like that?"

"No, Mr. St. Ives, I definitely wouldn't like that." He rose, picked up my cup, and poured me another cup of coffee, not forgetting to put in the sugar. When he handed it to me, he said, "I've never dealt with a professional go-between before."

"It'll probably be your last time," I said. "I don't have much repeat business."

"What I'm trying to ask, I suppose, is whether there's a code of ethics in your profession?"

"About as much as there is in yours, I'd say. My ethics are my own and they're not especially rigid or I wouldn't be in this business. But if they didn't protect the person who hires me—I guess I would call him a

34

client—then I wouldn't be in business. I haven't had too many complaints."

"I'm paying one hundred thousand dollars to insure my privacy."

I shook my head. "You're paying one hundred thousand dollars to stay out of jail. Your privacy, if you want to call it that, has already been broken. A lot of people know you're a thief, but none of them can prove it. Those journals can. If you want my guarantee that I won't peek inside once I get them back, I won't give it to you. I'm still too much of a snoop. But I can promise you that whatever I learn won't go any further than me. I don't know how I can make you believe that, but it's not really my problem. It's yours."

"Yes," Procane said, "I can see that."

"I should tell you that when Myron Greene first mentioned your name, I told him that I thought you were a thief."

Procane frowned. "Was that necessary?"

"Probably not, but it's done, and after my nice little talk about ethics, I thought you should know."

"What did Greene say?"

"He said he didn't care and that it was all hearsay anyhow. Actually, I think Myron likes having a thief for a client."

Procane looked at his watch. "It's now ten forty-five. The man said he would call at eleven to give you instructions."

"How'd he sound when you talked to him?"

"A little nervous, I think, but I couldn't really tell because his tone was strange."

"How strange?"

"Tinny."

"He probably used a distorter," I said. "They've all learned about voice prints from TV so distorters are the latest thing."

Procane nodded as if he knew all there was to know about distorters, and then said, "Do you always work alone?"

"I do now," I said. "I tried working with someone else a couple of times and both were disasters."

"Comegys—the Frenchman I spoke of—encouraged me to work alone whenever possible. But he also told me that as I grew older I would learn of certain opportunities that I'd have to forgo because they were too complex for one man and I would discover there was really no one I could trust. I remember him saying, 'Find someone and train them just as I found and trained you.' Two years ago I finally took his advice. I've acquired two associates, a young man and a young woman. They're quite efficient, even brilliant, I think. If you should need assistance, feel free to call on them."

"I'll keep it in mind," I said and then we sat there in a not uncomfortable silence until the phone rang. After Procane said hello, he handed me the phone and I listened carefully. Whoever was on the other end was using a distorter all right and the first thing he wanted to know was whether I had the money.

"I can get it," I said.

"Okay, now listen good, because this is gonna be a little complicated. In fact, you may want to write it down."

"Go ahead."

"There's an all-night laundromat, the coin-operated kind that almost never has an attendant, over on Ninth Avenue between Twentieth and Twenty-first. It's called the Neverclose. You got it?"

"I've got it."

"Okay, now here's whatcha do. You get one of those airline bags and put the money in it."

"Ninety thousand," I said.

"Yeah, ninety thousand. I'm letting you take your ten percent off the top so that means you're kinda working for me, right?"

"Right."

"Well, put the money in the bag," he said and then paused as if giving me time to write that down.

"How do you want it?" I said. "Fifties, twenties, tens, or what?"

"Fifties and hundreds will be okay," he said, "just so they're old. Hell, a hundred-dollar bill's nothing anymore."

"Okay," I said, doing some rapid calculation. "It's going to weigh about three and one-fourth pounds."

"Is that all?" He sounded a little disappointed.

"That's what sixty thousand dollars in fifties and thirty thousand in hundreds will weigh."

"If that's all it's gonna weigh, then throw in some tens. Say ten thousand in tens."

"That'll be another two pounds," I said.

"Okay. Now at three A.M. sharp tomorrow, Sunday morning, you walk into the Neverclose laundromat. You got that? Three A.M."

"I've got it."

"At five minutes past three put the airline bag in a dryer. I don't care which one. They got six of them and they're the spin kind. They also got a heat control on them so make sure the heat's turned down low. You with me?"

"All the way."

"Okay. Now after you got the airline bag inside the dryer, close the door, and put a dime in at exactly six minutes past three A.M. Sharp. Now at exactly seven minutes past three A.M. one of the other dryers is gonna end its twelve-minute cycle. I don't know which one yet, but one of them will. Okay. So you open it up and take out what looks like a blanket, only the blanket's gonna be wrapped around the five ledger things I've got. You still with me?"

"Sure," I said.

"Okay. Now you got four minutes to look at the ledgers to make sure they're for real. Then you got one minute to leave. I'm gonna be watching. But if I try a double cross all you gotta do is wait for the dryer that you put a dime in to finish its twelve-minute

37

cycle and then you can take your money back. How do you like it?"

"Wonderful," I said. "Real clever."

"I spent a lot of time thinking it up. It protects you and it protects me. You want I should run through it again?"

"No," I said. "I've got it."

"Okay," the tinny voice said. "I'll be watching just like I said so if you got any funny notions about putting cut-up paper in that bag, forget about it."

"I don't work that way."

"Yeah, I know," the voice said. "That's why I asked for you. But maybe I should mention that I got some Xeroxed copies of the stuff and it makes real good reading."

"What are you going to do with the copies?"

"Nothing, if everything goes off like it should. If it don't, I'll mail em to the cops."

"How do I know you won't anyhow?"

"You gotta learn to trust somebody someday, St. Ives," he said and hung up.

After I put the phone down I told Procane what the thief wanted me to do. He nodded a couple of times while I spoke and when I was through he said, "What do you think?"

"It's not bad, just a little overly elaborate with the dryers and the split-second timing. But it'll let him observe me and keep us from bumping into each other. What about the money? It's Saturday."

"Yes," Procane said, "that does present a problem. It's going to take me several hours to arrange for it."

I made a list of the denominations I wanted, but I didn't ask how he was going to arrange for a hundred thousand dollars on Saturday. I suppose people who are worth a million or so can do things like that. On weekends I have a hard time cashing a check at my hotel for twenty dollars, but I've only lived there six years. Procane, however, didn't seem at all concerned about raising one hundred thousand dollars. Maybe he planned to steal it.

6

I thought about my first and only meeting with Abner Procane as Myron Greene showed off his driving skill by speeding up Sixth Avenue as fast as the early Sunday-morning taffic and the red lights would allow, which was about eighteen miles per hour. The fancy car reflected another of his semisecret desires: Myron would like to have been a gentleman racing driver.

When we got to Forty-fifth Street I said, "I've changed my mind. I don't want to see Procane until I get rid of this jailhouse smell."

Myron Greene sniffed. "You weren't really in jail."

"It smells that way."

"It must have been—uh—uncomfortable."

"Confining, too."

Myron was explaining how my last comment could be taken as a joke when he drove up in front of the Adelphi and stopped.

"Thanks for getting me out of jail," I said and started planning my escape from the cockpit of the de Tomaso Mangusta whose midmounted engine popped and spat as it idled at what sounded to me like thirty-five hundred revolutions per minute.

"I must confess that I rather enjoyed rousing those people out of bed at four-thirty in the morning," Greene said. Being a topflight criminal lawyer was another of his occasional fantasies.

I finally found the lever that opened the car's door and it only took another fifteen seconds to figure out how I could swing my feet onto the sidewalk without rupturing something. "Thanks for the ride," I said.

"Be sure to call Procane," said Myron Greene, the worrier.

"If there's somebody else who now wants to sell him back his journals, they can wait till I take a shower."

I had to bend far down from the waist to see the dubious nod that Greene gave me as an answer. Then I slammed the door shut and watched him streak off toward Darien and the $165,000 home that he called a bungalow.

Indifferent, I suppose, was the best word to describe the atmosphere at the Adelphi Hotel because its food, service, and maintenance lay somewhere between fair and awful. The only time the place showed any zip was around the tenth of the month if you hadn't come up with the rent.

The hotel catered to permanent guests such as myself who lived alone and didn't demand too much in the way of service. The guests were mostly widows with rather large pensions and very small dogs; a few UN diplomats who didn't entertain much; three or four industrious call girls who were on the wrong side of thirty and trying to sock a little away; several peripatetic businessmen who muttered to each other in the elevator about the rotten state of the economy, and a couple of rich, quiet alcoholics who smiled a lot and didn't bother anyone.

The hotel also offered a bar and grill and restaurant called the Continental that had to depend on total strangers for its survival.

Caring for the wants and whims of the guests was a true son of Manhattan, Eddie, the bell captain. He was somewhere in his forties and owned a couple of tenements in Harlem and a taxi that was driven by his two brothers-in-law. He also ran a short string of call girls, accepted all bets, and answered all questions,

40

including those about the weather, in a whisper that bordered on the conspiratorial.

I carried the blue airline bag over to the desk and watched the day clerk lock it away in the safe. Eddie was waiting for me by the elevator.

"You look like you had a big night," he said.

"Did you get that jack-o'-lantern to my son?"

"Yeah. You done a good job on it. The kid was real tickled."

"You saw him?"

"Sure I saw him. I wasn't gonna turn a ten-dollar pumpkin over to just anybody."

"What did he say?"

"Aw, it wasn't what he said, it was the way he looked. You know how kids are."

I nodded, entered the elevator, and went up to my empty "deluxe" efficiency apartment to see whether I could wash away the precinct grime. I tried to think of something better to use than soap and water, but I couldn't come up with anything.

I spent at least twenty minutes under the shower, for some reason thinking about the night before when the hundred thousand dollars had been delivered to me by the man and the woman who, if they'd been only a few years younger, I would have thought of as the boy and the girl.

They had knocked at the door about nine-thirty. I was in my favorite chair half-watching a movie on television and half-reading all about Mr. Thomas Gradgrind of Coketown in *Hard Times,* a novel that I had never been able to get all the way through. I put Dickens down for what must have been the hundredth time and went over to open the door. The man carried the blue airline bag slung over his left shoulder. He kept his right hand deep in the pocket of his topcoat. The woman stood slightly behind him and to his left, the side that the money was on. He looked at me for a while as if trying to decide whether my face went with the description that someone had

41

given him. He apparently decided that it did because after a moment or two he said, "Do you always open your door like this, Mr. St. Ives?"

"Except when I'm in the shower," I said. "Then I don't open it at all."

"I'm Miles Wiedstein. This is Janet Whistler. Mr. Procane sent us."

"Come in," I said.

After they were in they looked around the place as if automatically checking to see whether there was anything worth stealing. I looked, too, and was mildly surprised to find that there wasn't. The TV set was black and white and more than five years old. The books were mostly paperback, except for the blue leatherbound Oxford edition of Dickens. The best piece of furniture in the place was the poker table, which I also ate on. The silver wasn't silver at all; it was stainless steel, and I wouldn't have been embarrassed by an earnest offer of nine hundred dollars for everything.

Wiedstein removed the airline bag from his shoulder and placed it on the poker table. "We'd like you to count it."

"You want a drink or a cup of coffee while you watch?"

Wiedstein looked at Janet Whistler. She shook her head no. "We're fine like this," he said.

They didn't quite stand over me while I counted the money, but they watched. Carefully. There were a few new bills, mostly hundreds, but not enough to cause any bother. It was all there and when I finished counting, I said, "Do you want a receipt?"

"That would be nice," Janet Whistler said. She was attractive enough if you liked tall, rangy girls with slender figures and easy, natural movements. I didn't mind them. She wore a loose gray-tweed coat that ended just above the black, over-the-calf boots that had to be laced all the way up to the top. Her hair was straight, brown, and shiny and fell halfway down her

42

back and sometimes into her eyes so that she had to keep brushing it away. Her face had pleasant features, although some might have called them sharp. I thought of them as finely chiseled—except for her mouth, which was a bit on the wide side. Her eyes were a deep, dark brown and I don't think she wore any makeup, but nowadays I have a hard time telling.

I crossed over to the typewriter, took its cover off for what must have been the first time in three weeks, rolled in a sheet of paper, and typed: "Received from Miles Wiedstein and Janet Whistler, One-hundred-thousand dollars ($100,000)." Then I typed in my name and the date, rolled the paper out, signed it, and gave it to Wiedstein. He read it, nodded, and handed it to the girl. I decided that he was twenty-four and she was twenty-three.

While she read it, Wiedstein said, "Mr. Procane told me to ask whether you were quite sure that you won't be needing any assistance tonight?"

"I take it you're the ones who're in that on-the-job training program of his."

Wiedstein smiled at that, a brief, even fleeting smile, but one that lasted long enough to show that there had been a concerned orthodontist somewhere in his childhood. Although his looks wouldn't turn any heads, he was tall and seemed fit enough and the length of his light-brown hair wasn't anything to fret about, regardless of your taste.

"He insisted that we ask you," Janet Whistler said and handed the receipt back to Wiedstein. He stuck it away in the left-hand pocket of his double-breasted brown topcoat that had a sheepskin collar. The coat looked warm.

"Tell him that it was nice of him to ask, but that I won't be needing any assistance."

Wiedstein let his eyes wander over to the money that lay stacked on the poker table. "Your share's ten percent of that, right?"

"Right."

"Let me know when there's an opening on your staff."

"Dissatisfied with your present setup?"

He shook his head. "Not at all. Yours just seems to be a pleasant business. Low risk and high pay."

I looked at him for a moment or two and decided that his gray eyes weren't set too far apart after all. His nose just had a wide bridge. "If you study hard with Procane," I said, "we might do a little business someday."

"We might at that," he said and turned to Janet Whistler. "Let's go."

She smiled at me and I smiled back and together they moved toward the door. When he had it open, Wiedstein turned and said, "I'd be a little more careful about opening my door, if I were you, Mr. St. Ives. You never can tell who'll be on the other side of it."

"You mean thieves," I said.

Both of them smiled again. "That's exactly who I had in mind," he said. "Thieves."

When they had gone I went over to the poker table and counted out ten thousand dollars. It made an impressive looking stack. I counted it again to make sure that I wasn't cheating anyone, especially myself, then looked at it some more and decided that it was far too much money for one night's honest work.

By the time I took it downstairs and locked it away in the hotel's safe, I had convinced myself that what I had to do that night wasn't all that honest.

44

7

There were four of us waiting for the phone to ring in
Procane's office-study that Sunday afternoon. Procane
sat behind his desk. Janet Whistler, wearing a dark-
green pantsuit, was in a chair in front of the desk, and
Miles Wiedstein and I were in the chairs that flanked
the fireplace. We were waiting for someone else to
call and for the second time tell me where I should
deliver ninety thousand dollars so that Procane could
get his journals back and stay out of jail.

The phone rang at four-thirty and both Procane and
I jumped. The ring didn't bother either Janet Whistler
or Wiedstein and I decided that they must have had a
good night's sleep. Procane picked up the phone, said
hello, then listened, said just a moment, and handed
the phone to me.

I said hello and a man's voice said, "St. Ives?"

"That's right."

"It's just like I told Procane this morning. I'm offering the same deal, just a different time and a different
place." He was using a distorter, but not a mechanical
one. It sounded as if he had a couple of marbles in his
mouth. In addition to that, he seemed to be trying to
strain his voice through something—a handkerchief
perhaps or even a washcloth. It made him difficult to
understand and I was glad he hadn't decided to pile
on a Chinese accent. Some of them do.

"When and where?" I said.

"Tomorrow morning at ten o'clock—"

"Tomorrow at ten's out."

"Why?"

"A couple of homicide detectives want to talk to me about Bobby Boykins and how he got killed. You knew Bobby, didn't you?"

There was a brief silence and then the voice said, "Okay, Monday's out. We'll make it Tuesday at ten."

"Where?"

"West Side Airlines Terminal, you know where it is?"

"Tenth and Forty-second."

"Okay, at ten o'clock you go upstairs to the men's room. Go in the first crapper stall on the left. If it's busy, wait till the guy comes out. Then go in, sit down, and wait. Have the money in that same Pan-Am bag. Just wait there until somebody comes into the crapper stall next to you. They'll push an airline bag under the partition into your stall. At the same time, you'll push your bag—"

"Not at the same time," I said. "I'm going to look first."

"Okay, you look first. Then you push the money over. Then you get the hell out of the men's room and out of the terminal. And don't get any funny ideas about hanging around outside and waiting for somebody to come out of the men's room carrying a Pan-Am bag. By the time they come out of there, it won't be in there anymore. You got it?"

"I've got it."

"Now I'll tell you how I want the money."

"All right."

"In twenties and fifties. Nothing bigger."

"All right."

"And when you see those homicide cops tomorrow, St. Ives, I wouldn't mention anything about where you're going to be at ten o'clock Tuesday."

"You did know Bobby Boykins, didn't you?" I said.

There was a silence that went on for nearly ten seconds until it was broken by the click of the phone as he hung up in my ear. I put Procane's phone down and then told him what the distorted voice had told me.

Procane was silent for a few moments and then he said, "What did he say when you mentioned Boykins?"

"Nothing."

"Do you think he's the one who killed him?"

"Possibly."

"But you're not going to tell the police?"

"I don't have anything to tell them yet. I don't even know if Boykins was involved. All I know is that Boykins's dead body was found at a laundromat I happened to be visiting at three o'clock this morning."

"There must be some connection," Wiedstein said.

"Maybe. But Bobby Boykins was a small-time con man, not a thief. He wouldn't know how to steal a hub cap, but he knew a lot of people who do."

"You're suggesting that he might have been the thief's go-between?" Procane said.

I shook my head. "I'm not suggesting anything. But between now and Tuesday morning I'm going to nose around. I know some people who knew Boykins. They might have heard something. Whoever killed him worked him over when they really didn't have to. He was an old man. When you get that old you don't refuse to talk because you've learned that there's no percentage in it. The only reason that could have kept Boykins from spilling everything he knew was that he also knew that as soon as he did talk, he'd be dead."

Procane leaned back in his chair and looked at one of his paintings. This one showed a half-grown deer hesitantly leaving a sunlit copse. I decided that Procane liked to paint sunlight and that he did it very well. The deer was good, too. "It would appear that our simple transaction is becoming complicated, Mr. St. Ives," he said.

"Extremely so," I said. "But murder never simplifies anything, although that's why a lot of them are committed."

"I never thought of it in just that way." He paused, as if taking time out to give it a thought or two now. "I do believe you're right," he said after a moment. Then he shifted his gaze from the painting to me. "Are you still adamant about working alone?"

"Why?"

"You said that you might nose around in an effort to determine whether Boykins had any connection with the theft of my journals. I was wondering whether you would object if Miss Whistler and Mr. Wiedstein were to do the same thing, but perhaps from a slightly different approach."

"I don't mind," I said. "In fact, I wouldn't mind at all if they were hanging around outside the men's room at the West Side Terminal Tuesday morning. If I don't come out after twenty or twenty-five minutes, Mr. Wiedstein might even come in to make sure that I'm not lying dead on the floor of the first stall."

"Yes, I was going to suggest something like that," Procane said.

"Perhaps you should also mention the time element, Mr. Procane," Janet Whistler said.

He looked at her and then at Wiedstein who nodded his agreement. Procane cleared his throat the way some people do when they think they have something weighty to announce. "It's imperative, Mr. St. Ives, that the journals be returned to me by no later than Wednesday morning."

"I can't guarantee that," I said.

"Yes, I know. But should the person who called here today want to postpone the transaction, I must insist that you press for the time that we've agreed on."

"What if he stalls anyhow and I can't get them back by Wednesday morning?"

The three of them exchanged looks that left me completely out of whatever it was that they had to say to each other. "If that happens, Mr. St. Ives," Procane said, "then we'll have to take certain steps that may or may not involve you."

"I don't think I quite understand that," I said.

Procane smiled and I could see nothing but reassurance and confidence in the way he did it. "Let's hope that you won't have to," he said.

There's a bar on Forty-second Street just west of Ninth Avenue that's called The Nitty Gritty. A few years ago it was called The Case Ace and before that, The Gung Ho. Back during World War II, somebody told me, it had been called The Hubba-Hubba, but I didn't believe it. Although the name of the place changed every few years, the owner and the clientele stayed the same. The owner was Frank Swell and the clientele was composed of the losers who hang around that neighborhood. For the most part they were pimps and whores, thieves and shylocks, checkwriters and fences, and a varied assortment of down-and-outers who were always trying to borrow five till Friday. I'd never seen anyone lend them a dime.

Frank Swell didn't like his customers and he kept changing the name of his place in hopes that they would go away. Sometimes when I felt depressed I would drop into Frank's and after I left I invariably felt better because I knew that there was no real reason that I had to go back there unless I wanted to feel better again after I left. It had that kind of atmosphere.

At six o'clock that Sunday evening I was sitting at the bar listening to Frank Swell read off a new list of prospective names that he hoped might drive his customers away.

"Listen to these, Phil," he said.

"I'll take another Scotch and water first."

"Sure." He served me the drink and then started to read from his list. "The Chez When, The Third George, The Aquarius—that's sort of timely."

"Sort of," I said.

"The Blue Apple, Greenbeard's, The Triple Eagle, and here's one I like, The Blue Blazer."

"That's class," I said.

"Yeah, that's what I need. Something real classy, then these creeps maybe wouldn't come around no more."

"I've got one for you," I said.

Frank Swell whipped out his ball-point pen. "Okay."

"Swell's," I said. "Just that."

He didn't even write it down. Instead he shook his head, folded his list of names, and stuck them away in his shirt pocket. "Nah," he said. "That'd just help em remember. I want one that they don't like, one that's too classy for em so they'll feel uncomfortable, you know what I mean?"

I nodded and he looked around sourly. He was about sixty and he had owned the place for nearly thirty years. "Look at em," he said, twisting his thick, gray lips into a sneer that was almost a snarl. I followed his glance. There were a couple of whores at the far end of the bar. Three of the booths were occupied by couples, and only one of them wasn't fighting about something. There were two other men at the bar. One of them, a beer nurser, looked grim and gray and pale, as if he might have just got out of prison and didn't much like what he had found. The other man was in his late thirties, had a round face that smiled a lot, and dressed in a manner favored by some minor Boston politicians that I had once known. He wore a pale-gray, almost-white homburg and a dark-gray cashmere topcoat with a black-velvet collar. They didn't seem to go with his pastrami sandwich. His name was Finley Cummins and he stole for a living and he had nodded and smiled at me when I came in.

I turned back to Swell. "The usual bunch," I said.

"You know what they are?" he said. "They're the dregs of humanity, that's what." He liked the phrase and it must have been the dozenth time he had used it on me.

"I thought Bobby Boykins usually dropped in about this time," I said.

Swell leaned his heavy arms on the bar. He had his shirt sleeves rolled up and his forearms were covered with thick hair that was turning gray. Just below his left sleeve was the fading red-and-blue tattoo of a shield that read, "Death Before Dishonor." Swell shook his head after I mentioned Boykins's name.

"Now there's a case for you," he said. "An old man like him who's drawing social security and still trying to con the suckers with the pigeon drop."

"He was still working it okay the last time I heard."

Swell again shook his head. "He's too old to be going around dropping a billfold in front of people. I mean it's not dignified."

"Have you seen him lately?"

"He was in here Friday late," Swell said. "I didn't talk to him but Cummins there did. You wanta know about Bobby Boykins, talk to Cummins. Another creep."

"I think I will," I said and moved down the bar to the round-faced man who was eating the last bite of his pastrami sandwich.

"How's it going, Finley?" I said.

Cummins licked his left thumb. "Best pastrami sandwich in town," he said. "That's the only reason I come in this crumb joint. What brings you around, St. Ives, slumming?"

"I thought Bobby Boykins might be here."

Cummins gave his thumb a final lick and then held it out as if he wanted to make sure that he had got all of the mustard off. "No you didn't," he said.

"I didn't?"

"Bobby got hisself killed early this morning over on Ninth Avenue. You should know. You were there."

"News gets around."

"You should know about that, too."

"Okay," I said. "I was there. How'd Boykins get so far out of his depth?"

51

"How should I know?"

"Swell said you were talking to him Friday."

"Hey, Swell," Cummins called without turning his head.

I looked down the bar at Swell who didn't look up from the Sunday comics. "What?" he said.

"You talk too fuckin much," Cummins called in a voice that could be heard all over the bar. Nobody looked up, not even Swell.

"You don't like it here, stupid," Swell said, still studying Dick Tracy, "go somewheres else."

Cummins turned to look at me. The smile was gone from his face. In its place was a frown, a suspicious one. "What were you doing down in Chelsea?"

"I was working," I said.

"A buy back? One of those go-between deals of yours?"

I nodded.

"How much?"

"Ninety thousand."

"Son of a bitch. The old bastard wasn't lying after all."

"Why?"

Cummins shook his head, still frowning. "I don't wanta get messed up in this."

"You won't," I said. "Not by me."

Cummins seemed to think it over. He looked at his empty glass. If he were going to tell me anything, I was going to have to pay something, even if it were only the price of a glass of beer. I ordered another Scotch for myself and another beer for Cummins. After Swell served them and went back to the comics, Cummins said, "Friday night he told me he had a hot one. He wanted me to go in with him."

"What else did he tell you?"

"That it would cost me three thou and that I stood to make fifteen."

"What did he want you to do?"

52

"Deliver something to a laundromat. Around Twenty-first and Ninth."

"He didn't say what it was?"

"He said it was hot. He said I could buy in half for three thou and make fifteen more just like that." Cummins snapped his fingers. "He said he paid six thou for it and that he was selling it back for thirty. He didn't say anything about ninety thousand though. Were you really carrying that much?"

I nodded. "Where'd Boykins ever get six thousand dollars?" I said.

"His brother died last August out in California. He left it to him."

"Did he tell you what he'd bought?"

Cummins shook his head. "He didn't talk much after I said no. But he told me who he bought it from."

"Who?"

Cummins looked at his beer glass again. It was empty. I started to order him another, but he said, "I ain't thirsty."

I sighed and said, "All right. How much?"

"Christ, if you're working a ninety-thou deal, you gotta be flush."

"It all comes out of my pocket, Finley. You know that."

"A hundred."

I shook my head.

"Seventy-five."

"Fifty," I said.

"Let's see it."

I took two twenties and a ten from my billfold and handed them to Cummins. He stuffed them into his topcoat pocket. "You ever hear of a guy called Jimmy Peskoe?"

"The name's familiar. He was a safe man, wasn't he?"

Cummins nodded. "One of the best. Or he was until they sent him up to Dannemora about ten years ago. He just got out. Well, somehow he hears about this

53

safe and he goes in and opens it up, but there ain't no money in it so he just grabs whatever there was. Then when he finds out what he's grabbed he gets all nervous. He done a bad ten years up there, I hear. So he sells it to Boykins for six thou. At least that's what Boykins said. But, shit, he lied a lot. That worth fifty to you?"

"It might be if I could talk to Peskoe."

"I ain't stopping you."

"Where could I find him?"

"I ain't information."

"Another ten for Peskoe's address."

Cummins gave it to me with a proper show of reluctance. It was a hotel over on East Thirty-fourth. He watched me write it down and when I was done, he said, "Was what you wanted to buy back really worth ninety thou?"

"At least three people thought so," I said.

Cummins turned that over for a moment. "Boykins and the guy who was putting up the ninety thou are two. Who's the third one?"

"The guy who killed Boykins," I said.

Neither the ambulance nor the cops had arrived yet, but a knot of people were already gathered in front of the cheap hotel on East Thirty-fourth when I got out of the cab. They were looking down at the smashed, sprawled body of a man. One of them was a skinny individual in his fifties who was coatless. I guessed he was the hotel clerk because he stared at the body and kept saying, "He was Mr. Peskoe and he was in eight-nineteen."

I turned to a tall, stooped old man in a thin black sweater who was picking his long nose and staring at Peskoe through thick bifocals.

"What happened?" I said.

The old man inspected something that he'd found in his nose and wiped it on his sweater. "Suicide, that's what. Some drunk probably." He looked at me, sniffed, and then stretched his mouth into a tight line of disapproval. "Lot of drunks around nowadays. In high places, too. Washington. Albany. Everywhere." He kept staring at me suspiciously so I looked away, over his shoulder, toward the entrance of the hotel.

If it hadn't been for the old man's suspicion, I might not have seen the man and the woman who hurried from the entrance and headed up Thirty-fourth Street, away from the body of Jimmy Peskoe. But I didn't have any trouble recognizing them. The man was Miles Wiedstein. The woman was Janet Whistler.

8

Two hours later Janet Whistler didn't smile or nod when I came into the Adelphi's lobby and walked over to where she sat in a brown club chair. She wore a long belted coat of dark-green leather and the same pantsuit that she had worn earlier in the day. She was smoking a cigarette and as I approached she snuffed it out with the air of someone who has smoked too many of them while waiting too long.

"I think we should talk," she said.

"My place or the bar? They're both private."

She hesitated just long enough for me to decide that a proper upbringing could still do occasional battle with the liberation movement. "The bar," she said.

It wasn't difficult to find a table because they were all empty. We chose one near the door and when Sid came over from behind the bar she ordered a bourbon and soda. I asked for a Scotch and water that I didn't particularly want or need.

"Where's Wiedstein?" I asked after we had tasted our drinks.

"He's picking me up here later."

"What's it like?"

"What?"

"Working with Procane."

"I like it."

"That doesn't tell me what it's like."

She started unbuttoning her leather coat and then shrugged out of it before I could help. "It's like nothing I've ever done before," she said. "But then I haven't done much."

"College?"

"Three years."

"You want me to guess?"

"Don't bother. It was Holyoke."

"Then what?"

"I drifted. A little modeling, mostly in Paris; some acting out on the Coast and here."

"How did you hook up with Procane, answer an ad?"

"Procane's analyst recommended me. I was seeing him, but not professionally. He told Procane that I had all the attributes of a cunning thief. We met, talked it over, and that's how it happened."

"What's Procane's problem?"

"Does he have to have one just because he's seeing an analyst? That's a terribly old-fashioned attitude."

"I've been told that I'm rather out of touch."

"Didn't you ever feel the need just to talk to someone? A person like Procane might feel that. Or perhaps he's just afraid of heights. Don't you have some secret doubts or fears that you'd like to talk to someone about?"

"Probably," I said. "Most people do."

"Well, that doesn't mean you're crackers, even if you do wake up some mornings and wonder why you're doing what you do, which I think is really a silly sort of a business."

"The hours are good," I said.

"Is it that or are you afraid that you couldn't hack it anymore at what you used to do? You wrote a column, didn't you?"

"That's right."

"And now you're doing something that's just a little shady, something that has just a bit of a smell to it."

"Some people think it's glamorous."

"But what do you think?"

"That its demands are just about right for someone without too much ambition."

"Like you?" she said.

"Like me," I said and smiled to show that I wasn't taking any of it very seriously.

She swallowed some more of her drink and said, "Someday we'll have to talk about what made you run out of ambition."

"All right. Someday we will. But you wanted to talk about something else. What?"

"Jimmy Peskoe," she said and then watched me carefully.

"What about him?" I said.

"You know him?"

"I've heard of him."

"He's dead."

"So?"

"We think he's the one who stole Procane's journals."

"We?"

"Miles and I."

"What makes you think so?"

"Miles found someone Peskoe was trying to sell the journals to."

"Who?"

She shook her head. "That's not important. He's reliable. He says Peskoe was willing to sell them for ten thousand dollars."

"But he didn't buy?"

"No."

57

"Did he know what they were?"

"Not really, but Peskoe said he should get a hundred thousand for them."

"Why didn't Peskoe do it himself?"

"He was too nervous."

"Not too nervous to be a thief though."

"That takes a different kind of nerve."

"Why didn't the guy buy the journals from Peskoe?"

"Simple," she said. "He didn't have the money."

"And you say Peskoe's dead?"

"That's right."

"When?"

She looked at her watch. "A couple of hours ago. He jumped, fell, or was pushed from his hotel. Room eight-nineteen of the Joplin Hotel. It's on East Thirty-fourth."

"You were there?"

"Just after he jumped. Or was pushed or—"

"Fell," I said. "What did you do?"

"It happened just before we got there so we went over to look at him. We didn't know who it was then. A few seconds later the desk clerk came out and said it was Peskoe and that he was in eight-nineteen. He kept saying it over and over. So we went into the hotel and lifted the key to eight-nineteen, took the elevator up to the tenth floor, walked back down, and then went through Peskoe's room. The journals weren't there."

"Did you find anything else?" I said.

Her eyes had brightened when she told me about it. She must have liked the excitement. Searching Peskoe's room had taken nerve, I had to admit, although I didn't much want to for some reason, probably because she thought I was in a silly business. I was almost beginning to agree when she said, "We didn't find anything. What else could there have been?"

"Six thousand dollars," I said and felt a bit smug.

"What six thousand?"

"The six thousand that Bobby Boykins paid Peskoe for the journals."

The excitement went out of her eyes and it was replaced by a kind of thoughtful reappraisal. At least that's what I interpreted it to be when she said, "You're not quite as indolent as you look, are you? Maybe you'd better tell me about what you've been up to."

So I told her about the unsuccessful approach that Bobby Boykins had made to Finley Cummins and how Cummins had furnished me with Peskoe's name for a price and how Peskoe was lying dead on the sidewalk when I arrived at the hotel on Thirty-fourth Street.

"What do you call these people you talk to," she said, "'contacts?'"

"I just think of them as friends and acquaintances."

"It didn't take you long."

"It doesn't when you know where to ask. You found out about Peskoe and it didn't take you long either."

She shook her head. "We're in the business." She said it seriously and I didn't laugh at her perhaps because she really felt that there was honor among thieves, especially the kind who had spent three years at Holyoke.

"It doesn't matter how we found out," I said, "because all we know is that Peskoe probably stole the journals from Procane and probably sold them to Bobby Boykins who got killed before he could collect on them for ninety thousand dollars. We don't know who's got the journals now. Whoever has them probably killed both Boykins and Peskoe."

Something was bothering her so she decided to ask me because there was no one any wiser around. "Why would they kill Peskoe?"

"You found out that Peskoe was trying to peddle the journals to at least one other person besides Boykins. And I found out that Boykins was trying to sell a share in them to at least one person. God knows how many

59

others the two of them approached, maybe half a dozen. So maybe one of the ones that they approached decided to cut himself in without putting up any cash. So he killed Boykins and took the journals. And maybe Peskoe knew who it was—or at least could figure it out. So Peskoe jumped out of his window, or fell, or was pushed."

"Mr. Procane isn't going to like this at all," she said.

"Is that where Wiedstein is now—telling him?"

"Yes."

"He should have waited."

"Why?"

"Then he could have told Mr. Procane how much I don't like it."

9

Detectives Oller and Deal didn't much like it Monday when I wouldn't tell them the name of the person who had handed me ninety thousand dollars to deliver to a laundromat at three o'clock in the morning.

"What have you dreamed up, St. Ives," Carl Oller said, "some kind of go-between's code?"

"Nothing so fancy," I said. "It hasn't got much to do with morals and ethics. It's just how I make a living. If I talk too much, I'll be out of business and then I'll have to go look for an honest job and I'm too old for that."

"You're not even forty," Frank Deal said.

"I feel old."

We were in one of those small, brown interrogation rooms at Homicide South and I'd already been there for an hour. Deal and Oller had taped my statement first, a brief, bare, formal one that was studded with facts, and now they were asking the informal questions, the ones that I didn't have to answer unless I wanted to, and I was being choosy.

"You know what we could do, don't you?" Oller said. "We could charge you with failure to report a felony." He said it in a tone that didn't carry much conviction, probably because he didn't believe it either.

"No you can't," I said, "because you're not sure that one's been committed. All you know is that I was delivering ninety thousand dollars to a laundromat and happened to stumble across a dead body. I don't have to tell you where I got the ninety thousand. And I don't even know whether Boykins was supposed to get it. Maybe he was, but I'm not sure."

Deal took a package of Pall Malls from his shirt pocket and shook one out, lighting it with a wooden match that he struck beneath the table. He inhaled some smoke, blew it out, and then carefully wiped some imaginary dirt from the top of the table with his right hand.

"Bobby Boykins was working on something big," he said. "Big for him anyhow. We heard that around. He'd come into a little money and he was trying to parlay it into a big score."

"I don't see how that affects me."

"If you'll tell us who your client is and what he wants to buy back, then we can probably connect up with who killed Boykins and why."

I shook my head. "You expect me to say no to that, don't you?"

"We don't know what you might say," Oller said. "That's why we keep asking you dumb questions. We figure you might come up with some smart answers."

Oller stood leaning against the wall to my right. He wore a dark blue suit. Its shiny elbows and narrow lapels meant that it was at least five years old. His coat was open and his white shirt bulged out over his belt. He wore a red-and-blue tie that had a small dark stain on it just below the knot. He dressed like a man who had too many kids and not enough money.

"Anything else?" I said.

Deal brushed some more imaginary dirt from the top of the table. "There's not too many rules in your business, are there?"

"Not too many."

"I was just wondering if you got any rules about how you're supposed to feel when some poor old guy gets killed who didn't mean two hoots in hell to you or anybody else. You got any rules about that, St. Ives?"

I stood up. "No, I haven't got any rules about that."

"That's all we're trying to do, you know," he said. "Just find out who killed some poor old bastard who didn't mean a shit to anybody. We're not trying to put you out of business or anything."

I started toward the door and stopped. "You get some proof that Bobby Boykins was supposed to collect that ninety thousand dollars and maybe I can help you."

"Maybe," Oller said as if he didn't like the word. He looked at Deal. "You know what?"

"What?"

"Someday we're gonna get a call from somebody who's been shot or stabbed or both and probably stuffed into some car trunk. And then we're gonna go out and open up the trunk and guess who it'll be?"

"Him," Deal said.

"I wouldn't be at all surprised. I think St. Ives is gonna get one of these go-between deals and he'll be delivering a little bag full of money somewhere, maybe trying to buy back some jewelry, and he'll run into some hardnose who's decided that he's got a big need for both the jewelry and the money. That's when they'll call us in."

Deal leaned across the table toward me, his hands

clasped tightly in front of him. When he spoke, he spoke to Oller, but he looked at me. "There's one other thing," he said.

"What?" Oller said.

"When we start looking around for who killed St. Ives, you know what I hope?"

"What?"

"I hope that everybody we talk to is gonna be just as nice and cooperative as he's being here today."

Oller smiled. "Yeah, that would be nice, Frank, wouldn't it?"

Outside I caught a cab and gave the driver the address of a restaurant on Lexington between Fifty-fifth and Fifty-sixth. The restaurant wasn't crowded and I ordered a martini and a club sandwich. The first drink went down so well that I ordered another one and when the sandwich came I asked for a glass of milk. By the time I'd ordered coffee, the young executive crowd had moved into the place. They wore colored shirts and bright, wide ties and suits whose jackets had lots of buttons and nipped-in waists. Although their clothes were a little gaudier than those of the late fifties and early sixties, their look of desperate confidence remained much the same. I decided it was the look of men who're sure that they have to be back at the office by two, but who are never quite sure why.

There was no desk waiting for me, so I called for the check, paid it, went outside, and leaned against a light pole trying to decide what to do with the rest of the afternoon. A cab came by and I hailed it and got in. The driver had to ask twice before I could think of somewhere I wanted to go. But after I told him the Joplin Hotel on East Thirty-fourth, I wasn't really sure that I wanted to go there at all.

You would expect to find the Joplin Hotel down near the railroad station, if New York had been a smaller town. It was the kind of place whose twelve stories had been built to accommodate the old-time

63

commercial traveler who didn't have a draw, depended solely on commissions, and wasn't quite sure what an expense account was.

You could almost predict what the rooms would be like from the looks of the lobby. They would be small with one window that stuck in the summer and refused to close all the way in the winter. They would have a steam radiator that clanked a lot around five in the morning. There would be a sink in one corner, but all that came out of the hot-water faucet would be some choking gasps. There would be a chair and a floor lamp with an orange shade and a forty-watt bulb. There would be a narrow bed with a thin mattress, springs that shrieked, gray sheets, and a pillow not much thicker than a magazine. If there were a television set, it would be the coin-operated kind that got only one channel.

The lobby had a high ceiling, a few worn chairs, a sagging sofa, a television set that didn't work, and the fiftyish room clerk who yesterday had stared down at the body of Jimmy Peskoe and repeated over and over that he had lived in room eight-nineteen.

The room clerk didn't move anything but his pale eyes as I approached the counter that he leaned on, supporting his chin in the palm of his right hand. When I stopped in front of him, he said, "You don't want a room."

"No."

"You wanta ask some questions about the guy who did the jump out of eight-nineteen. Peskoe."

"I could tell you that I was his brother."

"You could tell me that."

"But you wouldn't believe me."

The clerk moved his eyes up and down, as if assessing how much I had paid for my $150 topcoat. They were pale-blue eyes that I thought had a hurt look about them, as if they had seen too much—or perhaps not enough, and never would now that they were stuck behind the reception counter of a cheap hotel.

"No," the clerk said, "I wouldn't believe you."

"What if I said I was just nosey?"

The clerk seemed to think about that. He made his fifty-year-old face go into a frown. His gray upper teeth bit down hard on his thin lower lip. The only thing in his face that wasn't working was his tiny nose so he used his left hand to pull on that a couple of times. "You're not a cop," he said. It wasn't a question so I didn't say anything.

"You could be a reporter," he said. "You sorta look like a reporter—or what a reporter thinks he oughta look like. You know, when guys get your age they've pretty well made themselves look like what they are."

I thought about telling him that he looked like a philosopher, but decided not to. "I used to be a reporter," I said.

"But you're not anymore?"

"No."

"How much do reporters make nowadays, about three hundred?"

"About that," I said. "Some make more; a lot make less."

"I didn't think you was a reporter," he said. "You wanta know why?"

"All right. Why?"

"Because nobody's gonna send anybody who's making three hundred a week down here to ask questions about a nobody like Peskoe, that's why."

"You didn't like him?"

"What was to like? He stayed in his room. Eight-nineteen."

"How long did he stay here?"

The clerk yawned and didn't try to cover it up. The yawn gave me a good look at the inside of his mouth. His teeth were gray all the way back, except where they were black. Or the fillings were. His tongue was mostly yellow. There didn't seem to be much pink in his mouth. When he was through yawning, he said, "You know how I got this job?"

"How?"

"My wife kicked me out. So I checked in here because it was cheap. Then I got fired from my job and got behind in my rent so they let me work nights. For a while I tried to find another job, but who wants to hire anybody fifty-three years old?"

"I don't know," I said. "What kind of work did Peskoe do?"

The clerk was still wrapped up in his own problem. "I get my room and sixty-six bucks a week. Twenty-five of that goes for alimony. That leaves me forty-one a week and with withholding and social security that leaves me about thirty-five a week. Did you ever try eatin' on thirty-five a week?"

"It sounds tough," I said and pulled a twenty from my billfold and smoothed it out on the counter. It lay there for all of two seconds before disappearing into the clerk's pocket.

"Peskoe was here for a month," he said. "He didn't do nothing. I mean he didn't work. He just stayed in his room most of the time. He didn't have no visitors. He didn't get no calls or no mail. He just stayed in his room except when he went out to eat. Once in a while he'd go out at night. But not a lot."

"Did he drink?" I said.

"Nah. Maybe a pint a week."

"Then he wasn't drunk when he went out the window."

"He wasn't drunk."

"Did he seem depressed?"

The clerk looked at me curiously. "You with an insurance company?"

"Why?"

"I've heard if it's suicide, you guys don't have to pay off. On life insurance, I mean."

"I'm not with an insurance company."

The clerk seemed to believe me. He nodded a couple of times and then looked around the lobby. "You ask if he was depressed. He lived here, didn't he? We haven't got no happy guests. None I know of anyhow."

I brought out a package of cigarettes and offered the clerk one. He took it and I lit both of them. "What do the cops say?" I said.

The clerk shrugged. "Fell or jumped."

"Not pushed."

A crafty look went halfway across his face before it stopped and changed into greed. "Why would anyone wanta push a guy like Peskoe out of a window?"

I inspected the tip of my cigarette. "Maybe he owed them a little money and he wouldn't pay it."

That made sense to the clerk because he nodded a few times. "Maybe he owed you a little money, huh?"

"Maybe."

"And maybe he owed quite a few people a little money and maybe as long as he was alive there was a little chance that he might pay it off, huh?"

"Not a little chance," I said. "A big one. Peskoe was a safecracker. One of the best. Now do you understand?"

He started nodding his head again. "Now I get it," he said. "Now it makes sense."

It didn't, of course. But he was just smart enough not to want to seem stupid. "Did you notice anyone around just before Peskoe jumped or fell?"

The clerk lowered his eyes and started moving his finger back and forth across the surface of the counter. "Like I said, I make about thirty-five a week take-home and—"

"Here," I said and slid a ten across to him.

He pocketed the bill and then looked around the lobby. It was still empty, but he seemed to like the conspiratorial nonsense. "I ain't telling you anything I ain't already told the cops."

"That's fine," I said.

"There were two guys who went up just before Peskoe went out the window."

"Where'd they go?"

He shook his head. "I don't know. They coulda gone to eight or five or three. I don't know."

"They go up together?"

"They went up together."

"What'd they look like?"

He spread his hands in a gesture of defeat. "I don't know, I swear to God I can't remember. I saw em go up, but I didn't pay no attention. It's just like I told the cops, who pays attention in a place like this? All I know about em is what I didn't notice."

I sighed. "Okay. What didn't you notice?"

"I didn't notice em come back down."

10

The new batch of twenty-dollar and fifty-dollar bills amounting to ninety thousand dollars was delivered to me at 8 A.M. Tuesday at the Adelphi by Miles Wiedstein who this time accepted a cup of coffee while I counted the money and gave him another receipt. By 10 A.M. I was pushing my way through the entrance of the West Side Airlines Terminal's men's room, the blue Pan-Am bag slung over my left shoulder.

The first stall was occupied so I waited in front of it. A well-dressed man came out of the third stall down and saw me waiting. "Here," he said, holding the door open. "I'll save you a whole dime."

I shook my head. "I like this one," I said, pointing at the first stall.

"Christ, fella, a stall's a stall."

"Sorry," I said. "It's some kind of mental block. I can't go unless I use the first stall."

The man slammed shut the door he had been holding open. "You got a real bad problem there, don't you, sonny?" he said and walked out of the room before I could remind him that he hadn't washed his hands.

I stood there in front of the first stall, trying not to listen to the sounds and trying not to think much about why I was in a business that required me to stand there and listen to them at ten o'clock in the morning. Finally, at six minutes past ten the toilet in the first stall flushed and a small man of about sixty with a large nose came out zipping up his pants.

"I tried to hurry," he said apologetically. "I heard what you said about not being able to go except in the first stall. I'm like that at home, except that I can't go on the first floor. I gotta go upstairs."

"We both have a problem," I said and went through the door that he held open for me, thus saving another dime toward early retirement.

Once inside, there was nothing to do but sit down and wait. I waited four minutes until the stall next to me lost its occupant. Fifteen seconds later I heard its door open and close. I held the airline bag on my lap and kept my eyes on the space where the partition that separated the two stalls ended a foot above the floor.

I counted to thirty-five slowly and then a blue airline bag, this one from United, was kicked into my stall. I didn't see the foot that kicked it. I bent down and picked it up. I put my own bag on the floor. I unzipped the United bag and looked inside. There were five eight-and-a-half-by-fourteen-inch ledgers. I took out the first one and opened it at random. The entry was March 19, 1953. Written in blue-black ink in a precise, but somehow childlike hand was all the information that I would need to steal seventy-three thousand dollars from a Pittsburgh jewelry fence who talked too much to a girl in Manhattan. Everything was there: the time, the date, the method, and a virtual guarantee that the Pittsburgh fence would never complain to anyone. If it had been March 19, 1953, I might have been tempted.

I put the ledger back and took out another one and flipped through some pages. It was the same kind of information, but covered the five years from 1960 to 1964. I started to look at the rest of them, but there were three hard raps on the wall that separated the two stalls. I chose one more ledger at random and quickly flipped through its pages. This one was a complete blueprint of how I could have stolen myself fairly rich if it had been 1955 to 1959. I put the ledger back in the United bag just as three more raps sounded on the stall partition. They were not only louder, but also more impatient. I zipped up the United bag and then used my left foot to kick the Pan-Am bag that contained the ninety thousand dollars under the partition and into the next stall. Then I rose quickly, opened the door, and walked out of the men's room.

Miles Wiedstein stood to my right about six feet away, his right hand deep in the pockets of his topcoat. He looked at me and I nodded. To my left was Janet Whistler with her right hand tucked away in the large purse that she cradled in her left arm. I assumed that both of them had guns of some kind, but I wasn't interested enough to ask.

"Let's go," I said to Wiedstein.

"Did you get them?" he said and fell into step with me.

"Yes."

"Are you sure?"

"I didn't read every word, but what I did read convinced me that they were worth the ninety thousand —if Procane wants to stay out of jail."

Janet Whistler was on my left now as we went down

the stairs. "Shouldn't we wait to see who comes out of the men's room?"

I shook my head and kept on walking. "You can, but I won't. If the guy I gave the money to comes out and sees me, he may start shooting. Not right now, but later today. Or early tomorrow."

"You're sure you got them?" Wiedstein said again.

"There're five of them," I said.

Wiedstein nodded, but he still looked worried. Janet Whistler touched my elbow. "We have a car waiting," she said.

We went out the Forty-second Street entrance and into a waiting Carey limousine. All three of us got in the back seat and Wiedstein gave the driver Procane's address and then pushed the button that raised the glass partition. The car moved off and I settled back in the seat, the United bag on my lap, my arms clasped around it.

"Maybe I should have a look," Wiedstein said.

I turned my head and gave him what I hoped was a polite, but apologetic smile. "I'd better hold on to them until I can hand everything over to Procane."

Wiedstein stared at me for several moments before nodding thoughtfully. "Then you're assuming full responsibility," he said.

"That's my job," I said.

"He doesn't trust us, Miles," Janet Whistler said.

"That's too bad," Wiedstein said and then none of us said anything else until we were in Procane's office-study and I had handed him the United bag that had been kicked my way twenty-six minutes before.

Procane wore an old bluish tweed sports jacket, a pair of gray-flannel slacks, a dark-blue polo shirt open at the throat, and black loafers. He looked pink and well barbered and his hands shook only a little when I handed him the bag. He carried it over to his desk, unzipped it, and took out the five journals. He looked at me. "Did you check them?"

"Yes."

"How carefully?"

"Enough to know why you wanted them back."

He nodded at that and then sorted through the journals quickly until he found the one he wanted. He opened it and started turning the pages. His face grew pinker. He looked up at Wiedstein and shook his head. Wiedstein flushed and said, "Goddamn." Janet Whistler grimaced, crossed over to Procane, and put one hand on his shoulder. "Are you sure?" she said. Procane handed her the journal that he had been looking at. She flipped through it quickly and then tossed it on the desk. She said, "Shit."

Procane turned and walked slowly around his desk. His hand trailed along the edge of its top as if he needed support. He pulled out his high-backed chair and lowered himself into it carefully, the way an old man lowers himself into a wheelchair. The pink on his face had deepened into a dull red. He reached into a pocket, took out a vial, opened it, shook out a pill, eyed it thoughtfully, and popped it into his mouth. Then he looked at me.

"It is not your fault, Mr. St. Ives," he said.

Both Janet Whistler and Wiedstein turned to stare at me. From their expressions, they didn't seem to agree with Procane. He saw their looks and said, "It is not his fault. Definitely, it is not his fault." He sounded as if he were also trying to convince himself and not having too much luck.

"All right," I said, "whose fault was it?"

The three of them glanced at each other, once more exchanging some private information that they didn't seem to think was any of my business. Or they may have been taking a vote because Procane said, "Perhaps you'd better sit down, Mr. St. Ives. This may take a while. Would you like a drink?"

"I have the feeling I'm going to need one."

"Give Mr. St. Ives a drink, Janet," Procane said.

"Scotch and water, isn't it?"

"Yes."

Janet Whistler went over to a table that had some bottles and mixed a drink. She looked up once, but apparently both Procane and Wiedstein gave her a silent message that it was too early in the morning for them because my drink was the only one she mixed. After she handed it to me she found a chair near the desk. Wiedstein continued to stand, leaning against the wall near one of the oils that showed how Procane's Connecticut farmhouse looked on a sunny winter's day after about two feet of snow. I thought it looked nice and cozy.

All three of them were still gazing at me so I felt a little self-conscious about the drink, but not so much that I didn't take three deep swallows. After that I lit a cigarette, leaned back in my chair, smiled as pleasantly as I could at Procane, and said, "Okay, let's have it. Who fucked up what?"

The dull red on Procane's face had subsided to a faint pink. He ran his right hand through his ginger hair and then brushed his knuckles over his moustache. He looked around as if searching for something else to fool with, picked up the ledger that he had leafed through, looked at it for a moment, and then let it drop to his desk. It fell with a faint crash.

He looked at me and his lips worked as if they were practicing what he intended to say. "I should have taken you into my confidence, Mr. St. Ives. Because I didn't, I am in quite serious trouble."

"The ledgers are genuine, aren't they?"

"Yes, they're genuine. Did you have the chance to read much in any of them?"

"I read all about the Pittsburgh fence. I read about a few others, too. As receipts for a thief, they're extraordinarily detailed. And your planning would have to be described as meticulous, but writing it all down would have to be called dumb."

Procane's face took on a deeper shade of pink, but it disappeared quickly. "Writing it all down is part of the planning," he said. "It helps me to examine each one

73

objectively, discover possible errors, make needed changes. When I'm sure that I've planned as well as I can, I write everything down in here." He put his hand on the ledger. "Then I let it cool for a few weeks or even a month and reexamine it. It gives me a fresh perspective."

"It also cost you one hundred thousand dollars," I said. "But that's not what you're complaining about."

"Something's missing," Wiedstein said.

"What?"

"Four pages."

"From where?"

"From this journal," Procane said, again indicating the volume that he had let fall to his desk with the faint crash.

"That's the current one, right?" I said.

He nodded. "It covers 1970 to 1974."

"I noticed that it takes you about four pages to outline a single job," I said.

He nodded again.

"So four pages means that the plans or recipe for one theft are missing."

Procane didn't even nod this time. He simply looked at me and for a moment I almost thought that I was being let in on his system of silent communication. I stared back at him and my throat began to grow dry so I drank the last of my drink.

"When were you going to do it?" I said. "Next week? Next month?"

This time Procane shook his head slowly from side to side. "The planning for it has taken six months."

I rattled the ice in my drink. "All right," I said, "when was it set for?"

"Tomorrow," Procane said. "We are going to steal a million dollars tomorrow night."

74

11

"Good-bye," I said as I rose and headed for the door. Before I reached it, Miles Wiedstein moved in front of me. If I wanted to leave the room, I would have to ask his permission. I don't think he would have given it. I was about to ask anyway when he reached out and removed the forgotten glass from my right hand. "Let me fix that drink for you, Mr. St. Ives," he said.

I had to decide then between the door and the drink. But there was more to the decision than that and both Wiedstein and I knew it. I stared at him for a long moment as he stood there in front of the door, blocking my way without really seeming to. He gave me a small, polite smile and I returned it, noting that he was a little taller than I and a little heavier and quite a bit younger and no doubt in one hundred percent better shape. He made a small, inquiring gesture with the glass, probably reading my mind.

"Scotch and water," said St. Ives, the craven.

Seated once more in the chair in front of Procane's desk with the face-saving drink in my hand, I waited for someone to tell me why I should do something that I was sure I wouldn't want to do. Procane accepted the assignment.

"A million dollars, Mr. St. Ives, is a great deal of money."

There was nothing I could add to that so I only watched as he leaned back in his chair, clasped his hands behind his head, and again looked up at the ceiling. It was the act of a man who felt that he had something complicated to say and who needed to gather his thoughts before he said it.

"A million dollars," he told the ceiling, "is usually equated with success and happiness in this country. It's always been a rather mystical figure. If a man somehow acquires a million dollars, he should never again be financially insecure. Invested conservatively, it can provide him with an income of fifty or sixty thousand a year, which could be sufficient to his needs, even in New York."

He lowered his gaze from the ceiling, frowned a little, and then smiled briefly, the way a man does who has sorted out his thoughts so that they form a sensible pattern. "A thief's dream, of course, is to steal a million dollars. In cash. All at once. It's been done a few times. The Brinks robbery in Boston in 1950 comes to mind. The cash in that one was a little over one point one million. More than one and a half million was taken in 1962 from the mail truck in Plymouth, Massachusetts. And, of course, there was the great British train robbery the next year. That was worth seven million, I believe. Dollars."

Procane paused to shake his head as if in mild regret. "Many of these thieves were eventually caught, most of them before they could enjoy spending what they stole. Psychiatrists, of course, will tell us that they wanted to be caught, to be punished, as it were. I must confess that I have never suffered from that malady and I should add that I've explored it thoroughly with a most competent professional."

I wanted to make sure that I understood him. "You mean you've sought psychiatric help to find out whether you're the type of thief who has a subconscious desire to be caught?"

Procane raised his eyebrows. "Is that so surprising?"

"Yes. I'd call it that. Surprising."

"I became quite interested in the subject several years ago. I did as much research on it as I could.

76

After that, I put myself into the hands of an interested analyst and together we explored the entire question."

"And the answer was that you didn't have any problem."

Procane let his eyes wander over to one of his paintings. I followed the glance. The painting was of a tall old oak that rose from a forest clearing. It seemed to be spring, but the oak looked dead, killed either by light or age. Once again Procane had caught the sunlight well. Bright shafts of it seemed to bounce off the oak. He looked at me again.

"None of us, of course, is without problems," he said, "but a subconscious desire to be caught is not one of mine. Nor, I think I should add, is it a problem of either Mr. Wiedstein or Miss Whistler."

"The same guy checked me out," Wiedstein said, a grin brightening his face. "If that's what you call it. He already knew that Janet was okay."

"There's something that bothers me," I said.

"What?" Procane said.

"You say you steal only from those who won't go to the law. I've been trying to think of a crook that you could steal a million from."

Procane smiled. "Have you come up with any?"

"I'm still working on it."

"If the problem were only stealing a million," he said, "the most logical victim would be an armored-car company. I sometimes wonder about those firms' personnel practices. The majority of their help seems totally incompetent. Take last fall, for example. An armored car was hijacked and that really started me thinking about how best to steal a million."

"In Queens?" I said.

He nodded. "The truck had three guards who were delivering cash payrolls to three large firms. The guards stopped around six in the morning at a diner and two of them went in for coffee. The third remained in the truck. When one of the guards in the diner came back to let the one in the truck go for coffee, the thieves struck. Three of them. They made off with the truck, the two guards, and four hundred and six thousand dollars. What I marveled at was the laxity of the guards and the brilliant simplicity of the theft."

"The thieves later switched the money to a couple of cars and nobody's heard from them since," I said.

"And they won't," Procane said, "unless the thieves become careless."

"Or unless they want to get caught," Janet Whistler said.

Procane nodded. "Exactly. But if they don't, there's only a slight chance that they'll be apprehended through the efforts of the police or the FBI. Only one chance in twenty, in fact, according to the latest figures."

"I'm sometimes surprised that more people don't try it," I said.

Procane opened a desk drawer, brought out a clipping, and tapped it with a forefinger. "According to this story in the *Times*, only four point three percent of reported burglaries and four point two percent of reported grand larcenies result in arrests. Not convictions, mind you, but arrests."

"That means the average thief has a ninety-five percent chance of success," I said. "Not bad odds."

"Better than those that are faced by the man who wants to start his own business," Procane said. "But the odds shift dramatically when you want to steal a million dollars. I'd say that it's far more difficult to steal a million than it is to make it honestly. Especially if you want to steal it from someone who won't, as you say, Mr. St. Ives, go to the law."

"That could present a problem," I said.

Procane nodded again. "After considerable thought, I came up with two possibilities," he said, caught up in what seemed to be an earnest admiration of his own cleverness. But then I wouldn't have called him dumb. A little twisted, yes; a fool, no.

78

He was staring at the ceiling again. "I was limited, of course, to an illegal transaction in which a million dollars in cash changes hands. One possibility was a deal involving illegal armaments or gun running. The second, of course, was narcotics. I chose the latter."

I started shaking my head. I remember thinking that I should stop, but for some reason I couldn't. "You're going to try to knock off a million-dollar heroin buy," I said, and went on shaking my head. I must have been trying to indicate that I wanted no part of it. Not then. Not ever.

"Let him finish, St. Ives," Wiedstein said. "That's how I felt at first."

"I don't even want to hear it. I've been around some of the people who're big in heroin. Not close, but near. I've heard things. Those people are different. They've got something missing. I'm not talking about what they do, I'm talking about how they are. How they see things. You'd be better off stealing from the FBI. You'd have a better chance."

While I talked, Procane smiled patiently, as if he'd already given careful consideration to every point I had to make and had found nothing about any of them that should cause him the least bother.

"Planning, Mr. St. Ives," he said, wagging a cautionary forefinger. "You must not forget planning. Six months of it have gone into this theft. No detail has been overlooked. Seventy thousand dollars has been spent on securing information alone."

"Write it off," I said. "Cut your losses and take a long trip. Florida's not bad this time of year. Not too crowded yet. It could be a lot of fun. I might even go myself."

"I'm afraid that's impossible," he said.

"Why? You don't really need the money. You've already stolen your million, not in one chunk maybe, but over the years. Now you want to go up against the bunch that wholesales heroin. And you know what they are. They're condensed evil. I'm not talking about the nickel bag pushers up in Harlem or for all I know over in the next block. I'm talking, goddamn it, about an outfit that'll track you down if it takes ten years. And I could get bad nightmares from just thinking about what they'll do when they find you."

Procane nodded and looked interested and polite, as if I were the age of reason's local representative, but he really didn't need any. "If my journal had been returned intact, I might agree with you completely. Now I have no choice but to go ahead with my plans."

I rose and leaned across his desk. I started calmly enough, but by the time I was done, I was yelling. "At least three persons have already had their hands on your journals. The guy who stole them went out of an eight-story window. The old crook he sold them to was found dead in a laundromat. God knows who they talked to before they died. But maybe two dozen people know all about how you intend to steal a million dollars. You may have spent a lot of time and money developing your plan, but right now it's not worth a dime because it's probably old stuff all over New York and half of Chicago."

"Shut up and listen, St. Ives," Wiedstein said. "You could learn something. Not much, but something."

I sat back down. "All right," I said. "I'll listen. I don't know why I'm listening because I don't think that I really want to hear what you're going to tell me, but I'll listen anyway."

"Very well," Procane said. "You must realize, Mr. St. Ives, that when my journals were stolen I immediately realized that there was a possibility that they would be used for more than blackmail. My fears grew when I learned of the deaths of the Boykins person and of Peskoe, the safecracker. When you returned the journals to me with the four pages missing, my worst fears were confirmed."

"You'll have to admit that Boykins and Peskoe might have talked to a lot of people," I said.

"No," Procane said. "I don't think so."

"Why?"

"Because the four pages *are* missing. That means that whoever has the pages must know that neither Boykins nor Peskoe talked and probably made sure that they didn't. That's why they were killed."

"You're sure?"

"I'm sure of only one thing. That whoever has the four pages is going to make use of them."

"How, by blackmailing you some more?"

"That's one of three possibilities. But further blackmail would be possible only if I went through with the theft, don't you agree?"

I nodded and said, "What're the other two possibilities?"

"One is that whoever has the pages could use them to tip off the outfit from which I intend to steal the million. The drug merchants, as you call them. They might do this for a reward or simply to curry favor. Do you also agree to that?"

"It could happen," I said.

"The final possibility is the one that will dictate my actions. I've decided that it's the course that will be taken by whoever has the four pages because it offers the most profit and the least risk. Almost no risk at all."

He paused, perhaps to let my curiosity grow. It did. I was still something of a snoop. "All right," I said, "what is it?"

"I'm convinced that whoever removed the four-page outline from my journal will follow it to steal the million dollars himself—or rather themselves, because my plan calls for more than one person."

"Why remove it from the journal?" I said. "Why not just copy it out or even Xerox it?"

"First of all," Procane said, "they wanted me to know that they have it."

"To keep you from going through with the theft yourself?"

81

He nodded. "That's one reason. But you noticed, of course, that my journals were in my own writing?"

I nodded. I could see where he was going now.

"Well, earlier you predicted that the drug merchants were going to be terribly upset about having a million dollars stolen from them."

"I don't think I said terribly, but maybe I should have."

"Now suppose that you are a drug merchant who's just been robbed of a million dollars. And suppose you receive a four-page handwritten, detailed outline of the theft along with a note suggesting that the handwriting should be compared with that of one Abner Procane. What would you do, Mr. St. Ives?"

"If I were the drug merchant?"

"Yes."

"I'd have you dead by sundown."

12

Procane went on for another fifteen minutes about why he was convinced that whoever had blackmailed him out of one hundred thousand dollars was now going to steal a million more from some drug combine and blame everything on him. He built a solid enough case although I couldn't help but wonder how high his analyst rated him on the paranoia curve.

After a while I grew tired of listening and said, "Okay, you've sold me. Now why don't you just tip off the federal cops and let them nab everyone red-handed—the smugglers, the dealers, and the guys who're going to steal the million and blame you for everything."

Procane gave his head a small stubborn shake. "I have a considerable financial investment to protect."

"That's not it."

"No?"

"No. The real reason is that you want to be a million-dollar thief. I've been listening to you for almost an hour and I'd say that the whole thing has become an obsession. You want to join the thieves' hall of fame. You want recognition so bad that it's distorted your thinking."

The room grew quiet. Procane made a careful examination of his right thumb. Wiedstein discovered something interesting about the rug. Janet Whistler found a painting that she liked. The silence put on a little weight. It had grown fat by the time Procane said, "There's a kernel of truth in what you say, of course."

"You'd better tell him and get it over with," Wiedstein said, still examining the rug.

Procane ended the inspection of his thumb, used it to smooth down his moustache, and said, "Yes, I rather think you're right."

For a moment or two I thought that we were going to get another fat silence, but Procane said, "We'd like you to join us, Mr. St. Ives."

I didn't hesitate. I said, "No chance."

"Not as a participant."

"Still no."

"But as a witness."

"It's against the law."

"You would be adequately compensated."

"Not enough to die."

"The risk would be minimal."

"I'd make an unpleasant cripple."

"I was thinking of around twenty-five thousand."

"I'll listen."

"That's all I ask."

I still maintain that it was curiosity, not greed, that kept me from walking out. After all, I had just earned $10,000. In addition, there was $327 in my checking account and earlier in the year I had purchased $5,000 worth of highly touted common stocks that were still worth around $900 the last time I had looked at the financial page. So I was flush enough and therefore silly enough to listen to some thief tell me how he planned to steal a million dollars.

Actually, all three of them told it. When one of them dropped the story, another would pick it up and tell it for a while. Each of them spoke in the same flat, matter-of-fact tone, as if their plan to knock over a million-dollar heroin buy was no more interesting than a week they had once spent together in Memphis a long time ago.

After deciding that a heroin transaction would be his most likely prospect for a million-dollar steal, Procane's next problem was to find one. It wasn't easy and it wasn't cheap. His first move had been to turn both Janet Whistler and Miles Wiedstein into addicts —in theory, at least. They found themselves a pusher and in two months bought enough from him to establish themselves as heavy users. After three months they claimed poverty and became pushers themselves, staking out a small slice of the upper East Side as their territory.

Their supplier was a Puerto Rican they knew only as Alfredo. Over the months they bought forty-six thousand dollars' worth of low-grade heroin from him with money that supposedly came from their customers, but actually came from Procane. They threw the heroin down incinerators.

They had to act and talk like addicts and to do this, they had to associate with addicts. "It was difficult at first," Janet Whistler said. "Later on I think we came to feel a little pity for them. It's not a good way to be sick."

It was Janet who eventually discovered the link

they needed, an impoverished South American diplomat, very minor, who liked to fly up from Washington for New York parties. She met him at one given by Alfredo, the Puerto Rican supplier. Still using that same flat, totally unemotional tone she described how in bed the diplomat liked to boast of one of his embassy colleagues who, he claimed, was very big in the heroin smuggling trade. She said that it took a lot of time and a lot of care and an immense amount of flattery to get enough details out of him to make sure that he knew what he was talking about. Shortly after they became convinced that he did, the diplomat hinted that something big was about to happen. So Janet and Wiedstein set him up.

It was the usual arrangement, nothing fancy. Wiedstein burst into the hotel room and started snapping pictures of the diplomat and Janet without any clothes on. Wiedstein then threatened to send the pictures to the diplomat's ambassador, who also happened to be a brother-in-law, unless the diplomat found out everything he could about the next heroin delivery planned by the colleague who supposedly was very big in the smuggling trade.

"Our diplomatic friend almost panicked," Procane said tonelessly, "but he came up with the information." He got it by mounting a twenty-four-hour bug on his colleague's home phone. "The tape he furnished us was mostly in Spanish and mostly in coded references," Procane went on, "and it took me nearly forty-eight hours to break it, but when I did I was sure that we had the information we needed."

"He was nervous as hell," Wiedstein said. "He kept calling me every thirty minutes or so from his hotel here wanting to know if the information was solid. After we decided that it was I went by and picked him up and drove him to LaGuardia where I handed him ten thousand dollars for his efforts and a set of the pictures to remember us by. He was so grateful I thought he'd bawl."

Procane nodded approvingly at Wiedstein and then looked at me. "So, Mr. St. Ives, for an investment of approximately seventy-three thousand dollars—plus six months of our time—we have learned where and when we probably can steal a million dollars from certain persons engaged in the international narcotics traffic." He paused. "A most unsavory crowd, I assure you."

"You don't have to assure me of anything. What I'd like to know is how you want me to earn that twenty-five thousand you mentioned earlier. You said something about needing a witness, but that sounds a little fancy. What do you really want, someone to applaud when it's all over?"

Procane again clasped his hands behind his head and leaned back in his chair, letting his eyes roam around the ceiling. It was a position he seemed to like. "I think this is going to be a little harder for you to believe, Mr. St. Ives."

"That'll make it just like everything else I've heard today."

"I suppose every man who reaches my age suddenly realizes that he is not, after all, immortal. And it is around this time that many of us, I should think, look back and ask, is this all there is to it, or even, where did I go wrong?"

Procane paused for a moment, his eyes still on the ceiling. He looked reflective, Janet Whistler looked embarrassed. Wiedstein looked bored, as if he had heard it all before. Often.

"These middle-aged reflections sometimes lead to renewed bursts of vigor," Procane said. "This may account for what I consider to be the rash of menopause babies. Have you noticed it?"

"I haven't paid much attention," I said.

"The statistics are interesting."

"I'll take your word for it."

"These heretofore childless parents are actually having their last crack at immortality."

"All right."

"In effect, they're saying, 'remember me.'"

"You, too."

"Yes, me, too, Mr. St. Ives."

"The million-dollar score. It'll be preserved in the *World Almanac*."

"There and other places."

"You can read about it in jail."

"I'll never read about it."

"Why?"

"It won't be reported until I'm dead."

"Ah," I said, probably because I felt that he wanted me to.

"You're beginning to understand."

"Sure. You want me to write it up."

"That's it."

"Then what?"

"Give it to me."

"And it'll be found among your effects."

Procane nodded. "In a leather binder, don't you think?"

"That would be nice. What about your friends here?" I said, indicating Janet Whistler and Wiedstein.

"Just change our names," Wiedstein said.

"Change us completely," Janet said.

I began to get interested. "For twenty-five thousand?"

"That's right," Procane said.

"A complete story about the theft, using your name but not theirs. Everything else factual."

"Correct."

"Why don't you do it yourself?"

"I want a professional job from a disinterested observer."

"When'd you come up with this idea?"

"I've been toying with it for some time," Procane said. "But I couldn't decide how to approach a writer."

"If you'd mumbled something about the twenty-five thousand, there'd have been a line of them halfway down the block inside of an hour."

"I need a discreet one."

"Twenty-five thousand will buy that, too."

"Aren't you interested?"

"Sure, I'm interested. If you're still alive when it's all over, just give me a ring. You can either tell me about it or tape it. I'll write it up and even furnish the leather binding. Morocco would be nice."

"I admired your style when you wrote your column," Procane said. "I'm sure you could do an excellent job."

"Something like the one that was done on Robin Hood."

"I don't want a—what is it called—a puff piece."

"Of course not. You want a straightforward, factual account."

"I want a little more than that, Mr. St. Ives."

"What?"

"I want an eyewitness report."

"My eyes?"

"Yes."

"You're not serious."

"Quite serious."

"What am I supposed to do, peep around your shoulder while you jam a gun into somebody's ribs and note the deadly earnestness of your tone when you say, 'Okay, pal, this is a stickup'?"

"It will be quite a story, won't it?"

"Somebody else can write it."

"There's more to it than the little I've told you."

"You've already told me too much."

Procane smiled. "This will be my final operation."

"'The Last Score.' I'll give you the title free."

"What will happen to the money could be quite interesting."

I felt myself weakening and hated it. "What?"

"I don't really need it, of course," Procane said.

"I'm quite wealthy, so half of it—less the expenses I've already incurred—will go to Miss Whistler and Mr. Wiedstein as a kind of a bonus that will mark our severed relationship. After this final operation, they'll be on their own."

"And the other half million?"

"I'm not sure you'll believe me, so you have my permission to have our mutual lawyer, Mr. Greene, confirm it. I think he should have completed the paper work by now."

"Paper work for what?"

"There's an organization up in Harlem that works with drug addicts."

"So?"

"Some time next week it's going to get a half-million-dollar contribution from an anonymous benefactor." He paused and said, "Me," and then grinned and licked his lips a little as if he found the irony of it all delicious.

13

I agreed to do it, of course. At first I told myself that it was because I needed the money. When that wore thin I tried to blame it on the junkies up in Harlem who needed a helping hand. But after I admitted that half a million dollars wouldn't even help cure Harlem's sniffles, although a few billion might make a small dent in its problems, I stopped kidding myself and faced the real reason. It wasn't pretty, but it was simple. The real reason that I said yes was because I wanted to be in on a million-dollar steal.

I suppose that basically Procane and I were something alike. He wanted to steal a million. I wanted to watch. Perhaps I wanted to watch him do it as much as he wanted to do it. There's something voyeuristic about all newspapermen, even those who leave the trade and go on to better things, such as embezzlement and loan sharking and public relations. Nobody held a gun on me. Nobody threatened me with exposure. All they did was offer me the chance and after I got through protesting enough to make it seem decent, I grabbed it.

I decided that Procane's story was just farfetched enough to have some truth in it. I long ago had given up any illusions I might have entertained about finding the good thief, yet I couldn't help but rate Procane a notch above the others I had dealt with although that was probably because he stole only money that had already been stolen in one way or another. Also his manners were better, which demonstrated, I suppose, that there wasn't much of the egalitarian in me as I had thought.

So it was a mixture of normal greed and abnormal curiosity that made me agree to become a thief. There was no point in calling myself anything else. It was a long way from Sherwood Forest and besides nobody can tell me that the Merrymen joined up because of a stricken social conscience.

Procane looked surprised when I said yes. He probably thought that it would take at least another five minutes to convince me and he may even have been a little disappointed that I didn't give him the chance to use up all of his arguments.

"So you agree?" he said.

"I think that's what yes usually means."

"And the terms are satisfactory?"

"Almost. You said twenty-five thousand. I'll take half now."

That didn't bother him at all. He opened a desk drawer and took out a square gray-metal box, the kind that you can buy at the drugstore for $1.98 to keep important papers in. He counted out $12,500 on to the desk in fifties and hundreds. They made a tidy little pile about an inch high. The three thieves looked at me. I thought Wiedstein had a faint sneer on his face, but it could have been only a sad smile. Nobody said anything. Finally, I rose, leaned over the desk, and picked up the money. As soon as I had it in my hands, I wanted to give it back. But I didn't. I made a roll of the bills and stuffed them into a trouser pocket. Then I sat down again.

"Well, now," Procane said. "I won't ask for a receipt."

"You wouldn't get it."

"No, I shouldn't think so."

"You're in now, St. Ives," Wiedstein said. "All the way."

"Not quite," I said.

The three of them looked at each other, once again demonstrating how nicely they could get along without words. Procane's face lost its normally bland expression. His mouth tightened, his eyes narrowed, and something happened to his chin. It seemed to grow harder. He suddenly looked like a thief. A mean one.

"I think you'd better explain that," he said, his tone matching his look.

"Sure. I'm in, just like Wiedstein says, but I'm in for only what I was hired to do and that's watch. Nothing else. I'm not the utility man. If somebody gets shot, don't expect me to be the substitute getaway driver or carry the money or shoot back or anything else. I'll be an observer, but that's all. And if I think that's going to get me shot up or killed, I won't even be that. In other words, don't count on me for help of any kind."

Procane's face relaxed. "That's all we expect of you."

"Anything else and you'd just get in the way," Wiedstein said.

"Fine," I said. "Where will it be and when?"

"It will be tomorrow night as I mentioned earlier," Procane said. "As for where, I can only tell you that it will be in Washington."

"Oh," I said and there must have been something in my tone or my expression because Procane frowned and said, "I refuse to be more exact, Mr. St. Ives."

"Washington is exact enough."

"Is there something about Washington that bothers you?"

"I've had a little bad luck there. But so have a lot of other people."

"I see," Procane said, but I could tell from his tone that he didn't. "I'm sure you understand why I prefer not to tell you the details of our plans."

"Probably because I could sell them for a lot of money."

"I'm sure you wouldn't do that."

"But there's no sense in taking the chance."

He smiled. "No, there isn't, is there?"

I smiled back. We were all friends again. "Just tell me where you want me to be tomorrow and when."

He thought about that a moment. "Here, I think. Around noon?"

"Fine. Anything else?"

He looked at Janet Whistler. She shook her head. So did Wiedstein. Procane rose and held out his hand. "I'm delighted that you'll be with us, Mr. St. Ives. I really am." I accepted his hand and it still felt as though it belonged to a high school principal, but one who had a tough district.

"I'll see you tomorrow," I said.

"Mr. Wiedstein will drive you home. He's going that way."

"All right."

I said good-bye to Janet Whistler and Procane and followed Wiedstein from the room. We went out the front door and turned right on Seventy-fourth. "I'm parked around the corner," Wiedstein said. Around the corner we stopped at a dusty, two-year-old Chevrolet sedan. Wiedstein unlocked the curb-side door for me.

"I thought you'd have something fancier," I said.

"I don't need it," he said and I decided that his remark could be taken on several levels.

He drove well, making the lights work for him, and we were at Fifty-seventh and Park before he said anything else. Then he said, "I think you're nuts."

"For saying yes?"

"For even listening to him."

"Why?"

"Because there's a good chance you'll get mixed up in a shoot-out where somebody'll get killed. That means you'll be mixed up in murder."

"Does Procane's plan call for that?"

"No. He's never used a gun. Not to shoot anyone with. Not that I know of anyway."

"Why should he this time?"

"Because he may not have any choice."

"He must have taken that into consideration."

"He takes everything into consideration."

"You sound as though you're trying to talk me out of it."

Wiedstein glanced at me. "No, I'm just trying to convince you that you should be prepared for anything." He paused for a moment. "Anything," he said again.

"What about the people who're supposed to steal the million dollars and then blame it on Procane? What're they going to be doing all this time?"

"Doing what Procane's plan predicts they'll do."

"And what's that?"

"That's part of the plan."

"And you can't tell me that."

"No, I can't tell you that."

"Maybe you can tell me this. Does he use a computer to help him come up with his plans?"

"It's a lot like a computer, only it's better."

"What is it?"

"His brain."

We drove in silence for a while and then I asked, "What're you going to do with your share, retire at twenty-four?"

"Twenty-six."

"Well?"

"You don't retire on a couple of hundred thousand."

"You could try."

"I won't."

"You like your work, huh?"

"It's all I know."

"Where'd he find you?"

"Procane?"

"Yes."

"In a gutter." He looked at me and grinned sardonically. "Don't let the rough finish fool you, St. Ives. At nineteen I was graduating from Stanford. At twenty-one I was commanding an infantry company in Vietnam. At twenty-three I was in the gutter."

"It sounds like a lively tale."

Wiedstein shook his head. "Not really."

"What was it, drugs?"

"They don't do anything for me."

"A woman could have done it."

"Nothing so romantic. It was booze."

"You don't have the earmarks."

"You mean because I'm a Jew."

"That didn't cross my mind. Your age did."

"Jews aren't supposed to be drunks. They're supposed to have all this warm family support that keeps them from falling into the bottle."

"I've heard that theory."

"But you don't believe it?"

"I believe it's a theory that's used to explain why not too many Jews are alcoholics. But I've known some who were. Or are."

"Now you know another one."

"How bad is it?"

"Well, I've always been precocious. I made the whole thirty-year trip in less than three years. Blackouts. Convulsions. The whole thing."

"Where were you?"

"San Francisco and here. Procane found me in a gutter in the Village. He took me home with him."

I shook my head. Wiedstein glanced at me. "Sounds a little rich, right?"

"It doesn't sound like the way I think Procane should sound."

"He was looking for me. Or somebody like me. He got the idea from his analyst."

"Someday I'll have to meet that one."

"His analyst told him a bright, reformed drunk would make a hell of a thief. Procane's only problem was to find one young enough. He went looking and found me."

"But you weren't reformed."

"I was ripe though. Or thought I was. I lived at Procane's place for six months. He started teaching me what he knew. I wasn't too keen about it at first, but what the hell, I was broke and it was free room and board and a little pocket money. I kept sober for three months."

"Then what?"

"Then I got drunk."

"What happened?"

Wiedstein pulled up in front of the Adelphi and put the car in park. "Procane gave me one more chance. He made it clear that that's all it was. No lectures. Nothing. Then we pulled a job together and that was it. I was cured. That doesn't mean I can drink, but the compulsion's gone."

I must have looked dubious because Wiedstein gave me another sardonic grin. "Still sounds a little rich?"

I nodded. "A little."

"It's not really. It's just that I found out something about myself."

95

"What?"

"That I can substitute one compulsion for another," he said. "Now I'd rather steal than drink."

14

Myron Greene wouldn't even comment on the half-million dollars that was to be anonymously contributed to the Harlem drug abuse clinic, or whatever it was, until he checked with Procane to see whether it was really any of my business.

When he called back he said, "Well, it's just as Mr. Procane told you. He intends to contribute the money sometime next month and he's asked me to handle it. It's really no great problem although the tax aspect has some interesting angles."

"You mean it's deductible?"

"It's a little more complicated than that. It depends on how we decide to raise the money. There are capital gains to be considered and quite a few other technicalities that I won't bore you with."

"You're not boring me," I said.

"I fail to understand your interest, Philip."

"I'm just curious about whether you can make any money by giving away a half-million dollars."

"You can't make any money, but you can save a great deal on your current and future federal income tax."

"Give me a for instance."

"Well, Mr. Procane's income is such that it falls within what is called the fifty percent contribution base. In other words, he can contribute fifty percent of his income each year and claim it as a tax deduction."

"I aspire to that base."

"No you don't. Next we will probably decide to make the gift in the form of securities that have not appreciated in value since they were purchased."

"They'll be like those dogs that I bought."

"Yes, but I warned you about those. So, Mr. Procane will contribute a half-million dollars in securities this year. However, there is a special five-year carryover provision. This means that for the next five years he can deduct up to half of his income as a charitable contribution."

"So what do you think Procane makes each year, a couple of hundred thousand?"

"I'm not sure that's really your concern."

"He has to make that much to live like he does. So if he donates the half a million this year he can write it off during the next five years and it really won't cost him anything."

"That's an oversimplification."

"But essentially correct."

"Well, yes, I suppose so."

"He's all heart, isn't he?"

"I happen to think that it's an extraordinarily generous and worthwhile gesture."

"So does Procane. Good-bye, Myron."

I decided that it was still going to be a very long search for the good thief. The five hundred thousand dollars that Procane planned to hand over to the drug clinic was the five hundred thousand that he would have to pay anyway in income tax over the next five years. His half-share of the million he stole would probably be spirited off to Switzerland or Panama and cautiously reinvested from there. His tax diddle wasn't illegal, although stealing a million must be. But since he was stealing it from the drug merchants, I really wasn't sure what law Procane would be breaking, and somehow I didn't feel that Myron Greene was really the right person to ask.

It was one o'clock by the time that I got through talking to Greene. Before I could ask him about Procane's wonderful generosity, I'd had to tell him all about how I'd retrieved the journals, omitting no detail because he especially liked those.

Talking to Myron Greene usually made me hungry for some reason that I'd never bothered to think about so I decided on a Danish sardine sandwich which I created between two thick slices of dark German rye, and garnished with Bermuda onion, Dijon mustard, and Romaine lettuce. It was accompanied by a bottle of Filipino beer that had something of a kick to it. I was sitting there at the poker table, savoring the international flavor of my lunch and not at all worried about its gastric consequences, when somebody knocked at the door.

I took the last bite of the sandwich and swallowed the rest of the beer and with my mouth full I went to the door, put the security chain on, and opened it. I didn't recognize him at first because he wore a gray, double-breasted worsted suit with a neat chalk stripe and a blue shirt with longish collar points that framed the plump knot in his blue-and-white figured tie. His black, pebble-grained loafers were burnished and gleaming.

He could have been from the insurance company or even a high-class collection agency, but he wasn't. He was from the cops and the last time I'd seen him he had been wearing dark blue along with a pair of handcuffs that he'd locked around my wrists. He was Officer Francis X. Frann, once of the New York Police Department's motor-scooter patrol who, for all I knew, had now been promoted to plainclothes detective because of his brilliant work on the St. Ives case.

"Hello, Mr. St. Ives," he said.

I said hello, but it must have come out a little muffled after it went around the mouthful of sardine sandwich.

"I'd like to talk to you for a few minutes."

I swallowed and nodded, closed the door, took off the chain, opened the door wide, and waved him in. He moved to the center of the room and then turned slowly, his eyes sorting out the furnishings as if he suspected that most of them were stolen property.

"What have we got to talk about?" I said.

"I'm on my day off."

"I'm sorry."

"Why?"

"Your clothes. I thought you might have been promoted."

"That's why I'm here on my day off. I'd like to be."

"You're poking around in the Bobby Boykins murder."

He nodded.

"On your own."

He nodded again.

"That's nice. I wish you luck."

His eyes started to inventory my furniture again. They were still dark brown and they didn't look as if they cried easily. Somehow they didn't go with his twenty-four- or twenty-five-year-old face that was all pink and white with some light-blond eyebrows, a snub nose, a girlish mouth, and a prizefighter's chin.

When he got through checking out the furniture for the second time, he said, "I've got a friend or two down at Homicide South."

"It's nice to have friends. I'm going to have a beer. You want a beer on your day off?"

He hesitated a moment and then said, "Well, sure, a beer would be good."

I took two beers out of the Pullman kitchen's built-in refrigerator, poured them, and handed him a glass.

"Thanks," he said.

"Try that chair over there."

He tried the chair along with a swallow of his beer and said, "Hey, that's good stuff."

"It's from the Philippines."

He looked suspiciously at his glass, but took another swallow anyway. "Like I said, I've got a couple of friends down at Homicide South."

"What about them?"

"They let me take a look at that statement you gave Oller and Deal."

"So?"

"Well, it got me to thinking that maybe you knew more about this guy Boykins than you told Deal and Oller."

"It made them think the same thing."

"Yeah, I read their report, too. They said you weren't too cooperative."

"I'm sorry they feel that way."

Frann shook his head. "No you're not."

"All right. I'm not sorry."

"You wouldn't tell em who you were workin for."

"You're trying to bust this case by yourself, huh?"

"That's right. By myself. I never had a murder one right on my beat. There've been a bunch of manslaughters, but no murder ones."

"I'm glad things've picked up."

"It could give me a chance to show what I can do."

"I take it you want to make detective."

"I don't wanta stay on a motor-scooter, for Christ sake."

"And you think I can help."

Frann nodded his big chin a couple of times. "You can help all right, but it don't seem likely that you will."

"But you're going to try me anyway."

"I'm going to ask you some questions."

"Which I don't have to answer."

He shrugged and stretched out his feet in front of him. He seemed to be settling in for a long stay. "This go-between business you're in. It must make you a lot of money."

"Not so much."

"Oh, I don't know." He made his left hand perform a negligent wave. "Nice midtown pad, imported beer, poker table all set up, and ready to go. I imagine a guy like you plays table stakes."

"You've got a good imagination."

He nodded. "I don't think it's so bad. I imagine that on a deal like you were on the other night you'd make about nine or ten thousand dollars. I counted that money you were carrying, you know."

"So I heard."

"Money always makes me think."

"About what?"

"More money."

It was beginning to sound like a shakedown, but I wasn't sure. He was taking an awfully long time to make his point and most shakedown artists like to get right down to business and to hell with the social niceties. There was nothing to do but let him talk.

"I figured if I could find out who you were working that go-between deal for the other night, I might get a lead on who killed the old man."

"Uh-huh."

"So this morning I sort of followed you."

"Sort of?"

"I'm a pretty good tail. You didn't make me."

"That's right, I didn't."

Frann took out a small, spiral-bound notebook and flipped it open. "At nine thirty-three this morning you came out of here and caught a cab down to the West Side Airlines Terminal. You arrived there at nine fifty-one and then sort of fooled around outside. You were carrying a blue Pan-Am airline bag."

"I was meeting some friends."

"Huh. At ten sharp you went inside the building and then entered the men's room upstairs. You stayed in there until thirteen after ten. Then you came out

101

carrying a blue airline bag. But it wasn't no Pan-Am bag; it was a United one."

"You've got a great future on the force."

"That's when you made the switch—the buy back, wasn't it?"

"Whatever you say."

"I say this. I say you come out of the men's room and meet two people, a man and a woman. In their twenties, about my age. All three of you get in a Carey Cadillac limousine and then go to a certain address on East Seventy-fourth. You want the number?"

"No."

"It took me a little while to check this out, but that address is where somebody called Abner Procane lives. I couldn't find out nothing about him yet. But that's who you're working for, I bet."

"Doing what?"

"Making a payoff for him this morning. Buying him something back."

"What?"

"Well, Christ, I don't know that yet."

"You don't even know that I'm working for him. For all you know he's an old friend. I met two people at the airline terminal this morning. Maybe they'd just come in on a flight."

"They didn't have no luggage."

"Maybe they lost it."

"Yeah, well what about the airline bags? You take a Pan-Am bag into the crapper and bring a United one out. What about that?"

"I think you made a mistake. Or if you didn't maybe I did. Maybe while I was washing my hands I picked up the wrong one. Maybe the bag I took into the men's room contained some gifts for my friends and I didn't notice I'd picked up the wrong one until I got to the address on Seventy-fourth. You haven't got a thing, Frann, but a wasted day off."

His pink face got pinker. He rose and put the empty

glass down. "I'm gonna check this guy Procane out, then we'll see who made a mistake."

"You want some advice?"

"From you?"

"No charge."

"Okay, what?"

"If you check Procane out, don't check him out too hard. He's got a few million dollars tucked away here and there and I don't think you've ever had a few million dollars land on you."

"Money don't scare me."

"Then you've got guts all right. No brains, but guts."

Frann shook his head slowly and then smiled at me. I could find nothing friendly in it. "I haven't told you everything, St. Ives."

"But you're going to."

"I've been saving a little."

"Okay. What?"

"While I was waiting for you to come out of the men's crapper."

"Well?"

"Well, I seen who went in."

"And?"

"And a blue United airline bag went in at the same time."

"So?"

"So I happened to recognize the party that carried the bag in."

"But you're not going to tell me who."

He shook his head again. "No, I think this Mr. Procane would be a little more interested in that than you are." He turned toward the door and made it almost halfway there before he turned and grinned at me again with absolutely no humor. "Like I said, money don't scare me none. It don't scare me at all."

Then he was gone and I walked over to the phone and dialed Procane's number. When he came on I told him about Frann and what he'd said.

103

"What do you think?" Procane said.

"He might be trying some kind of a shakedown. I'm not sure. But I'm going to try to get him off your back. At least for the next few days. But to do that I'll have to promise something."

"What?"

"To reveal the name of my client. You."

"When?"

"Not before Friday or Saturday."

"Under the circumstances, I suppose it has to come out."

"I can stall it though."

"All right," Procane said. "Do what you think best."

After we hung up I called another number and then had to wait a minute or so before the extension I asked for wasn't busy. Finally, I got through and when I did a gruff voice that was almost a snarl said, "Detective Deal speaking."

"This is St. Ives."

"What do you want?"

"You've got a poacher."

"What's that supposed to mean?"

"You remember that young cop who was at the laundromat that night? His name's Frann."

"What about him?"

"He's using his time off to investigate Bobby Boykins's murder."

"Yeah," Deal said and put a little interest into the word, but not much.

"He's bothering me. I don't like to be bothered by snot-nosed cops."

"Jesus, that's really too bad."

"It's not just that I don't like it. What's more important is that my client might not like it."

"I feel sorry for him too. Whoever he is."

"Get Frann to stop bothering me and I'll tell you."

"You're beginning to interest me, St. Ives. What's Frann been doing to you?"

"For one thing he's been tailing me."

"When?"

"This morning—and I suppose this afternoon."

There was a brief silence and then Deal said, "When do you want to talk?"

"Friday is as soon as I can make it."

"Okay. Friday's fine."

"What about Frann?"

"Oller and I'll take care of him."

"Can I count on that?"

"As much as you can count on anything."

15

I took a risk, of course, when I called Deal to get Officer Francis X. Frann off Procane's back. It might have been worth a little money, or even a lot, for Procane to learn who Frann had seen going into the airline terminal men's room. Whoever carried the United bag in may have been a member of the team that had killed Bobby Boykins, thrown Jimmy Peskoe out of a hotel window, and was now planning to knock off the million-dollar heroin buy in Washington and then blame it on Procane.

But it seemed logical that if Frann had recognized whoever it was that had gone into the men's room, Oller and Deal would know all about it within a few hours—as soon as they caught up with Frann. A young rookie cop doesn't hold out information long from two seasonal homicide detectives, not if he likes his job. Or even if he doesn't.

And, too, once Deal and Oller found out who it was that Frann had spotted, they just might catch up with him in time to spoil whatever plans he had for stealing the drug merchant's million.

I spent the rest of the afternoon and part of the evening indulging in a mild bout of self-congratulation on how my cleverness and cunning probably had saved Procane no little money and much grief. I even made some notes that I felt might be included in the report that I'd been commissioned to write on the million-dollar steal. I was still feeling a little puffed up and debating about whether to open a bottle of fine $2.98 California champagne when the phone rang. It was Janet Whistler.

"Are you busy?"

"Not at all."

"I'm downstairs. In the lobby. And I'm hungry."

"Come on up and we'll figure something out."

When she took off her coat I saw that she wore a dark-blue dress that was low at the hem and high at the neck. Like most males, I was a fiercely partisan supporter of the miniskirt, but we seemed to be losing the battle to whoever it was that hated women enough to dress them up in clothes that made them look like they were all set to go duck hunting.

"I thought you'd be plotting far into the night," I said as I hung up her coat.

"That's all done. Procane believes in relaxing before a job."

"How does he go about it?"

"With Doctor Constable."

I must have looked at her questioningly as I moved toward the Pullman kitchen because she said, "Dr. John Constable. He's Procane's analyst."

"What would you like to drink?"

"How're your martinis?"

"They've drawn a few rave notices."

"I'll try one."

The secret of my martinis was that I didn't put any vermouth in them. None at all. Few seemed to care as

106

long as the gin was cold. I tried to stick to Scotch and water.

She sat in the same chair that Frann had sat in earlier that day and sipped her drink. She wrinkled her nose and said, "Straight gin?"

"I'm out of vermouth."

She handed the drink back to me. "Put a dash of Scotch in it. That'll kill the juniper berries."

I did as told and this time she nodded after taking another sip. "Fine."

"Procane's not having a session tonight, is he?" I said.

"No, they like to get together socially. Procane fascinates Constable. And as I told you, Procane needs somebody to talk to."

"About tomorrow?" I tried to keep the surprise out of my voice. I don't think I succeeded.

She smiled, but it seemed a little grim. "The sanctity of the couch. It's almost as good as the confession box."

"Where's Wiedstein?"

"With his wife and kiddies."

"I didn't know he was married."

"Very much so. He has three children. Twin girls, a boy, and a nice Italian wife who thinks he's New York's most dynamic life-insurance salesman. It gets him out of the house at night."

"That leaves only you without solace or comfort."

"I thought I'd come to the right place."

I put my drink down, rose, and walked over to her. "You did."

She took a swallow of her martini, a slow swallow, and then carefully set it on a table. I found the move stagey. What she really needed were some long gloves that she could begin to strip off in a careful, thoughtful manner.

She looked up at me and smiled and then smoothed her long hair back with both hands. Then she extended them toward me. "I don't need too much romancing," she said. "Just a little."

I drew her up and kissed her. It was a long, satisfying kiss and the gin that I tasted in her mouth had an erotic flavor to it. She stepped back, did something with her hands behind her neck, and then was out of her dress. She had nothing else on but pantyhose and she began to peel those off slowly, without shyness, as if she were a little proud of the effect that she knew it would have.

It took me a little longer to get rid of my clothes, but not much. Then we were locked together again, trying to devour each other's mouths, thrusting and squirming against each other, until she gave a little cry and shuddered and looked up at me.

"Hurt me a little first," she said.

"Where?"

"Here." She took my hand and guided it to where she wanted to be hurt. "Hard. Again." She gave another cry. "Oh, God, again! Please, please again!" So I hurt her some more because she wanted me to and she said, "Now with your mouth, please with your mouth, oh please."

Then we were on the rug between the chairs pounding down and up at each other and I felt her fingernails rake my back, which I didn't like because she did it again, making me plunge into her brutally and she said, "Oh my God, yes!" and now we came together, or at least almost together, subsiding slowly, and then she whispered, "I needed that," as if it had been a stiff drink rather than a stiff something else.

So it had been sex with plenty of lust, if not love or even liking, but since that was the only kind that I'd had for some time, I wasn't going to complain, not even about the raking fingernails. The act seemed to have been a kind of tonic for her and now neither of us owed each other anything except perhaps a fairly polite thank you, but maybe not even that.

She sat up after a while and slipped her dress over

her head, shivering a little from what must have been the cold. It couldn't have been modesty. "What do you think about chili?" she said.

"I have a certain amount of respect for it; at least my stomach does."

"I know an almost secret place that serves the best in town. I'll let you in on it because you're such a good fuck."

"You're not bad yourself."

"I know," she said as she pulled on her pantyhose.

I got dressed slowly in between swallows of my drink. She watched as she finished her martini which must have been warm, but she didn't seem to mind.

"How do you keep in shape?" she said.

"I don't."

"You look good. What are you, six feet?"

"Five-eleven."

"One-sixty?"

"About that."

"Diet?"

I shook my head. "I was born with a happy metabolism."

"Then you can eat chili."

"I can eat anything. It's only afterward that I sometimes wish I hadn't."

She looked around the apartment as if seeing it for the first time. "When I was up here before I didn't think this place looked like you. Now I do."

"I suppose that's some kind of a compliment."

"I mean the poker table and the three million paperbacks and the covered typewriter and all. It looked like a pose."

"For what?"

"For oh-so-carefully-casual."

"Oh."

"But you really are, aren't you?"

"Carefully casual?"

"No, I mean you just really don't give a shit."

"This place came with my alimony payments."

109

"What happened?"

"To the payments? She got married again."

"Any kids?"

"A boy. He's six."

"What's he like?"

"Smart. Like his mother."

"What was she like?"

"She was a nice girl."

"But a little ambitious."

"A lot of wives are."

"I'll bet she married money."

"A great deal of it."

"I'll also bet you busted up shortly after she found out."

"Found out what?"

"That you didn't want it bad enough to do anything about it."

"Money?"

"Yes."

"It wasn't only money."

"Social position then."

"Being married to a columnist is one thing; being married to a go-between is another. She thought it was a step down. A long one."

"What did you think?"

"I agreed with her."

"But you took it anyway."

"I told you I was a little short on ambition."

"But I didn't believe you; now I think I do."

"Maybe I should see Procane's analyst."

She looked at me—a little critically, I thought. "I don't think so. You're not freaky enough. He likes the real freaky ones, probably because he's so far out himself."

"How?"

She shrugged. "I went with him for a while. He had some funny kinks. Really weird."

"Such as?"

"Costumes, masks, that sort of thing."

"It didn't do much for you?"

"Not for me, but he liked it."

"Is he any good?"

"Professionally?"

"Yes."

"He thinks so." She paused a moment and then smiled. "He liked to dress up like Peter Pan best of all. Maybe that tells you something about him."

"I'll work on it. You want another drink?"

"No, not now."

"Then let's go find that chili."

It was nearly eight o'clock when we came out of the Adelphi entrance and turned left. We had decided to walk because the chili parlor that Janet Whistler had discovered was over on Fortieth Street, a little more than six blocks away. The weather was somewhere between crisp and cold and I remember thinking that a bowl of chili would taste good, even if I later had to ransack the medicine cabinet for something to put out the fire.

I spotted him sitting behind the wheel of the car that was parked in a no-parking zone. He didn't look at me and for a moment I thought he may have felt that if he remained absolutely still, it would make him invisible. The car was a three-year-old yellow Camaro with a 327 engine. I gave him a cheery enough wave, but he didn't wave back.

"Wait a minute," I said to Janet Whistler and tried to open the door that was next to the curb, but it was locked. I went around to the driver's side and tried that door, but it was locked, too. I noticed that the keys were in the ignition. The shoulder harness was strapped across his chest. His eyes were open and so was his mouth, the lips just slightly parted, but now that he was dead, they didn't look quite so girlish.

Janet Whistler was staring at him through the windshield. "Is he dead?"

"Yes."

111

"Who is he?"

"A cop called Francis X. Frann."

"Do you know him?"

"Yes and I think we're going to have to skip the chili."

She nodded. "Has he got anything to do with us?"

"A little. You'd better find Procane and tell him."

"What'll I tell him?"

"That the cop called Francis X. Frann is dead, that he's parked outside my hotel, that I'm going to have to call the cops, that Procane's probably going to have to talk to them some time tonight, and that he'd better be able to prove where he's been."

"Anything else?"

"You'd better scoot."

She nodded again, turned, and walked quickly up Forty-sixth Street. I went around in front of the car and wrote down the license number and the fact that it was a New Jersey plate. I went back up to my apartment and asked information for the number of Frank Deal. He lived in Brooklyn and a woman answered the phone. When I asked for Deal I could hear her call, "Frank, it's for you."

After he said hello I said, "This is St. Ives."

"Now what?"

"It's about Officer Frann again."

"Me and Oller haven't been able to run him down. Oller's here now. What's the matter, Frann still hanging around?"

"Sort of."

"Where?"

"He's in a car parked right outside my hotel."

"Well, hell, he can keep till tomorrow."

"He might even keep forever."

"What's that supposed to mean?"

"It means he's dead," I said and hung up.

16

A tow truck came for the yellow Camaro, an ambulance came for Officer Frann, and Deal and Oller came for me.

"They say he was stabbed," Deal said, "right in the heart." He and Carl Oller sat at the poker table. I wandered around the room, making myself useful by straightening pictures, lining up books, and chain-smoking cigarettes.

"Why don't you sit down, St. Ives?" Oller said. "You're giving me the jitters."

"Have a drink," Deal said. "You look like you could use a drink."

"I can," I said and crossed over to the kitchen to pour myself a Scotch. "You want one?"

"Not me," Oller said.

Deal shook his head. "Me neither."

I carried my drink over to the poker table and sat down. "All right," I said, "I've told you all I know about Frann."

"The way it looks to me is he was gonna try to shake down your client," Oller said. He was wearing a tweed sport coat that wouldn't quite button anymore because of his stomach. The jacket had gray suede leather patches on its elbows.

"And you haven't told us the name of your client," Deal said.

"Or what it was you were buying back for him this morning."

"Private papers," I said. "Personal stuff."

"It must have been goddamned personal if he was willing to pay ninety thousand bucks for it," Deal said.

"We're going to have to talk to him," Oller said.

I nodded. "That's what I told him."

"What'd he say?" Deal said.

"He didn't like it."

"But he agreed to talk."

"He agreed."

"When?"

"Tonight."

Deal looked at Oller who nodded. "Tonight's good. Who is he?"

I took a long drink of my Scotch and water. "His name's Procane. Abner Procane."

The two detectives looked at each other and then Deal shrugged elaborately, bringing his shoulders up high and dropping them. "Never heard of him."

"What kind of business is he in?" Oller said.

"Investments, I think."

"Loaded?" Deal asked.

"He's not poor," I said.

"I mean really loaded?"

"He's worth a few million."

"What I was thinking was if the kid wanted to shake him down for a few thousand, would it bother him enough to do something drastic about it, like sticking a knife in the kid?"

"I don't think so," I said. "I don't think he's much of a suspect."

"But you're gonna let us decide that, aren't you?" Oller said and gave me a slow smile to show how sweetly reasonable he thought his request was.

"Sure," I said.

"I suppose you can account for where you were this afternoon and evening," Deal said.

"Here."

"Alone?"

"Most of the time."

114

"Who else was here?"

"Frann for one."

"And for two?"

"A girl."

"And you were probably sticking it into her while somebody else was sticking it into poor old Frann."

"Probably."

"We may want her name," Oller said.

"I don't think so."

"You know something, St. Ives?"

"What?"

"We don't really give much of a shit what you think."

"Look," I said, "I've told you all I know. About the airline terminal, about the buy back and about who my client is. I'm not going to bring anybody else into this unless you charge me with something and I probably wouldn't even do it then."

"He's a real fuckin gentleman, isn't he, Frank?"

"Knock it off," Deal said. "What's this Procane's number?"

I told him and he said, "Is he home?"

"I think so."

Deal rose and crossed to the phone, dialed the number, and then identified himself. "We'd like to talk to you, Mr. Procane. I think St. Ives has told you why." He listened for a moment and then said, "Ten o'clock'll be fine," and hung up the phone. He walked around the room looking at pictures and books, even taking down a volume of Kipling's poetry and thumbing through it, perhaps looking for "If."

After a while Deal turned and said, "We got ourselves assigned to this one, St. Ives, because we're pretty sure it's tied into the Boykins killing. But Frann wasn't just some two-bit hustler who got himself beat to death. He was a cop and that means that we're not going to be working it alone. There's going to be a whole swarm of us because cops don't like cops getting killed. Am I making myself clear?"

"You're getting there."

"Well, what I'm telling you is this: if you haven't told us every goddamn thing about Frann that you know—I mean if you're keeping something back about him or about who might have killed him and then somebody finds out that you were keeping it back, well, you're going to be in one hell of a lot of trouble. I mean real bad trouble."

I thought a moment. "I told you everything he told me."

"But you're not sure he was really gonna try to work a shakedown?" Oller said.

"He didn't come right out and say so. He just said that he thought Procane might like to know who carried that United airline bag into the men's room this morning. I thought that if he were going to shake somebody down, he'd try it on the guy who carried the bag. But maybe he was planning to work both of them. Or it may even have been because of what he said was the real reason."

Deal had moved over to the door and Oller was joining him. They both stared at me.

"What real reason?" Deal said.

"That he just wanted to stop riding that motorscooter."

Procane called at midnight. "How'd it go?" I said.

"Not too bad; not too bad at all. They were very polite and very considerate, I thought."

"What did they ask you about Frann?"

"Whether I knew him and whether he'd approached me."

"What'd you say?"

"That I'd never heard of him. They must have asked me the same question a dozen times in as many different ways."

"Did they believe you?"

"They seemed to. Eventually."

"What'd you tell them about the journals?"

"That they were personal papers that could be embarrassing and that I could afford not to be embarrassed. So I bought them back."

"Did they ask to see them?"

"No, they seemed quite understanding although they said they thought that they could have saved me a lot of money if I'd gone to the police first. I tried to appear a bit crestfallen."

"Anything else?"

"I simply told them what had happened, how I came to get in touch with you through Myron Greene, and how you bought the journals back this morning after the previous attempt failed."

"How long were they there?"

"A full two hours. They just left."

"They took long enough."

"Well, they really were quite thorough. They asked me to tell the entire story several times and they examined the safe and looked around the house. Most conscientious, I thought."

"Do they want to talk to you again?"

"They said that they will. I told them I'd be away tomorrow and they said that that was all right because tomorrow was their day off. Or it's today, now, isn't it? Wednesday."

"And you're still going through with it?"

Procane's tone stiffened. "I really don't have much choice, Mr. St. Ives."

"No, you don't, do you."

There was a small pause and then he said, "I trust that you haven't had second thoughts about joining us."

"Not second thoughts. Mine are up in the hundreds."

"I really must know your decision now. The timing and logistics aren't such that they can accommodate last-minute regrets."

"When are we supposed to meet at your place?"

"At noon today."

117

It took a long time for me to reply because I had to run through each of the three dozen reasons why I should say no so I could decide on which one to use. But the next voice I heard seemed to belong to somebody else because I heard it saying, "I'll be there at noon."

17

I was thinking about getting a cat and calling it Osbert when the first gray light edged its way into the room. A cat would have been someone to talk to at ten past three in the morning when you know the night will never end. My watch said that it was a little after seven and the last of the longest night the world has ever seen. I knew it was the longest because I had measured every second of it. Twice.

It had been a while since I had seen a dawn so I got up and went over to a window and looked out. It was cloudy and it looked like rain and I decided that I hadn't been missing much.

On my way to the bathroom I turned on the burner under the kettle. I was going to need a lot of coffee that day to keep awake and I tried to remember if there were anything in the medicine cabinet that could help. A quick inventory produced a bottle of aspirin, a package of Stimu-dents (unused), a razor, a tube of Lip-Ice, a box of Band-aids, a bottle of Mercurochrome, a gift bottle of shaving lotion that I'd never used, and some foamy pain-killer that could be sprayed on minor burns. There was also a pill bottle with a label that read, "Take one every four hours if pain persists," but it was empty so the pain must have been persistent although I couldn't remember it.

After I found that there was nothing to put me to sleep, or to wake me up, or to make me feel any better, I said to hell with it and went back to the Pullman kitchen and fixed a cup of instant coffee and poured a shot of brandy into it. Drinking that early in the morning always made me feel wicked and that's exactly how I wanted to feel.

After the coffee I stood under the shower for a long time, shaved, and then cooked myself a large breakfast of three eggs, Canadian bacon, buttered toast with strawberry jam, a chunk of Liederkranz, and more coffee. Much more. By the time I was dressed in the dark-blue suit, blue oxford shirt, black knit tie, and black loafers—the outfit that I always wore to funerals and million-dollar heists—I was ready for a nap. I had some more coffee instead.

By eight-thirty I was not only breakfasted, dressed, and jittery, but also ready to go someplace. Even an office would have looked good. Instead, I turned on the television, which I considered to be almost as wicked as drinking in the morning.

I half-watched the news for thirty minutes or so and then some cartoons came on and I got really interested in one that was all about two bears and a tiger who spoke with a ripe Brooklyn accent. The bears seemed to be from the South.

The morning passed somehow, not quite as slowly as the night, but nearly so. At eleven I was jabbing the elevator button. When I came out of the elevator and into the lobby Eddie, the bell captain, shot his eyebrows up in surprise or maybe shock and said, "Christ, you're up early."

"It's not all that early."

"It is for you. You gotta lead on a steady job?"

"Not today."

"Well, one of these days something's gonna turn up."

"Let's hope so."

"You wanta get a little something down on the fight?"

"What're they giving?"

"Eight to five on the champ."

"I'll take him for eighty.'"

"I got some tickets I can letcha have for a hundred."

"Ringside?"

"They're a little further back than that."

"Ten rows?"

"More like maybe fifteen."

"Or twenty?"

"Nineteen."

"I'm going to be busy tonight."

"You got a date? That was a swell-looking piece you came out of there with last night. Maybe a little young though. For you, I mean."

"I'll see you, Eddie."

"Eighty on the champ, right?"

"Right."

I walked or rather strolled, I suppose, the twenty-eight blocks or so to Procane's house. It was windy and chilly and threatening to either rain or snow, but I decided that the walk would do me good. How, I wasn't quite sure, but that's what a walk was supposed to do. Everybody said so.

I celebrated the halfway mark by turning into a familiar bar and joining the morning drinkers in a Scotch and water. It was a good way to kill twenty minutes or so and for some reason I didn't want to arrive at Procane's early. On time or a little late, yes. Early, no.

I got there at five minutes past twelve. It had been a long morning. Procane met me at the door and once again ushered me into the office-study. He had a fire going; applewood from the smell.

"You're the first to arrive," he said after I took one of the chairs by the fire. He stood in front of it, his hands behind his back, rocking a little on his heels. He wore

120

a dark-gray suit, a white shirt, and a tie with black and white stripes. He looked as if he were headed for a meeting of the board and had some good news for its members. His eyes were bright and twinkling and a jolly smile kept peeping out from underneath his ginger moustache.

"I was about to have a drink, Mr. St. Ives," he said. "Would you care to join me? I don't think one will do us any harm while we wait."

I started to show off and say no, thanks, but common sense prevailed and I said, "Yes, I think I will."

After we had our drinks he sat in the chair opposite me and twinkled some more. "It must be a big day for you," I said.

"Yes, I believe it is. I've been up since six. You look as though you had a good night's rest."

"It was fine."

"Well," he said, raising his glass, "to luck."

We drank to that and then he said, "Of course, luck won't have very much to do with it."

"Planning," I said.

"Careful, exact planning with virtually every minute precisely scheduled."

"What if your—uh—victims, I suppose—what if they lag a little or move ahead of schedule?"

"Both contingencies are provided for."

Procane looked happy. There was no other way to describe it. He kept smiling and beaming even when there was nothing to beam about. He also seemed a little nervous. He kept crossing and uncrossing his legs, but it was the nervousness of anticipation, not apprehension.

I was curious so I asked him, "What do you like better, the planning or the execution?"

He seemed to think about it for a moment. "The execution really, although I'm rather hard pressed to make a choice between them. I hate to keep comparing it with painting but that's the only other thing that I do at all well. There's a great amount of pleasure in

121

the selection of a subject, in studying shape and form and color, and in planning my approach, but it never equals the feeling I get when I make that first brush stroke on canvas. After that it goes all too quickly. I paint very fast, Mr. St. Ives." He paused and twinkled some more. "I steal fast, too."

"What about afterward?"

"Afterward," he said thoughtfully. "Yes, that's a quiet time touched in both instances with a kind of melancholy, I think. The aftermath."

"Guilt?"

"Regret. Never guilt."

"When?"

"Only after a painting; never after a theft."

"Why after a painting?"

"I always have the feeling that somehow I should have done it better. I'm never quite sure how I could have done better, but there's always the nagging feeling that I should have. I never feel that way after a job."

"No remorse either? After a theft, I mean."

"I've never felt remorse about anything," Procane said and I found myself believing him. He paused a moment and looked thoughtfully at the fire. "As I've said, I've felt regret often enough, but never remorse because remorse implies guilt and I've never felt that."

"Did you ever wonder why? Nearly everyone feels guilty about something or other."

"I've thought about it and decided that it's probably because I'm content to be what I am—a master thief and a tolerable Sunday painter. I don't aspire to be anything—or anyone—else. I think a lot of guilt comes from people wanting to be what they assuredly aren't and can't possibly be. They feel guilty because they can't, but think that they should."

"How do you feel when you're stealing something?" I said. "I mean what are your emotions or do you have any?"

"Is this for the report, Mr. St. Ives?" he said and smiled as if he liked any conversation that was chiefly about him.

"Maybe."

"When I'm actually engaged in the theft—in the operation—I feel a kind of detached excitement. I know that I'm totally involved in what I'm doing and my powers of concentration seem enormously expanded. I'm conscious of almost every detail. And my recall after it's over is nearly total. I've sometimes toyed with the idea of painting a theft from memory. It might be interesting, especially one which involved a confrontation."

"Like the senator in Washington?"

Procane looked surprised. "Oh, do they know about that?"

"They had some strong suspicions."

"He was a totally corrupt man. Dead now. But he did look rather pathetic handcuffed to the radiator."

"I only read a couple of entries," I said, "but those journals of yours should be fascinating reading."

"To specialists in criminology or to the general public?"

"Both, I'd think."

Procane looked interested. "It would have to be done posthumously, of course."

"I'm afraid so."

"Do you really think there's a chance?"

"Myron Greene knows some publishers. He could handle it for you."

Procane's expression turned shy, almost embarrassed. "If it were published, do you think there's a chance of it being turned into a film?"

I managed to keep a straight face. "I should think so."

He was silent for a moment. "What do you think of Steve McQueen for the lead?"

"He'd be fine."

"Of course, Brando has a little more depth, I think."

"He'd be good, too."

The door opened before Procane could do any more mental casting. It was the only time I had seen him slip out of his role as the gentleman thief—poised, urbane, and almost witty. It was something of a shock to discover that he desperately wanted not only to see his journals published, but perhaps even more desperately he also wanted himself portrayed up there on the silver screen by Brando or McQueen or maybe, in a pinch, Lee Marvin.

It was comforting to learn that he had some failings and that they were distinctly human and not the weird kind that might go with the mad master criminal who liked to bake kittens in the oven.

Through the open door came Janet Whistler followed by Miles Wiedstein. I was interested in learning how one dressed for a million-dollar theft and so I was a little disappointed by Wiedstein's tweed sport coat, gray flannels, and dark-blue shirt open at the throat. At least his desert boots had gummed soles. He carried a thin black attaché case that he placed on the floor after he said hello to Procane and me.

Janet Whistler wore a dark-gray pantsuit and unremarkable black shoes. They both looked as if they had dressed up just enough to cash a small check at the corner liquor store.

They found chairs and Janet Whistler refused a drink from Procane. He didn't bother to offer Wiedstein one. Procane cleared his throat and said, "I called both of you last night about my visit from the police. I've concluded that their interest in me should not prevent us from going ahead with our plans, so we shall continue as scheduled."

"There're getting to be a lot of dead bodies lying around," Wiedstein said.

"We discussed that last night," Procane said.

"I just thought I'd bring it up again to see if St. Ives has any ideas."

"None except the obvious one," I said. "Whoever

killed Boykins and Peskoe could also have killed the kid cop, Frann."

"Yes," Procane said, "that seems logical on the surface. And it could also mean that they're the ones who're going to try to steal the million dollars and then tell the drug merchants to blame us."

"I don't see how you're going to stop them from doing that," I said, "even if you beat them to the million."

The three of them exchanged a few remarks with their eyes and Procane said, "I have decided, Mr. St. Ives, that I can only let you in on our plans one step at a time. I'm sure you understand why. But let me also assure you that every precaution has been taken." He stopped and then added, "Or will be within the next few hours."

He wasn't going to tell me anything until he thought that I needed to know it so I decided to stop asking. I was going along as the paid trained observer, the chronicler with an eye for the relevant detail, the biographer of a thief and his apprentices. I promised myself to remain cool, detached, and disinterested. A little Olympian even. I patted my pockets and debated about asking Procane whether I could borrow a pencil and something to write on.

He had turned to Janet Whistler. "You checked the shuttle flights?"

She nodded. "No delays to amount to anything."

Procane looked at his watch. "The limousine is outside?"

"He picked Janet and me up," Wiedstein said.

"Well," Procane said, "I think we should be going. Will you do the honors, Miles?"

Wiedstein picked up the thin black attaché case and opened it. It was a fitted case lined with what looked like black velvet. Nestled each into its own nook were four automatic pistols not more than six inches long with beautifully engraved slides.

The case was first offered to Janet Whistler who

took one, checked the magazine to make sure that it was loaded, and dropped it into her black envelope purse.

"A matched set, Mr. St. Ives," Procane said, selecting one. "They're seven-shot Walthers. The 1931 PPK model, although these are of quite recent manufacture and really most excellent." He tucked his away in an inside jacket pocket that may have been specially tailored because I detected no bulge.

Wiedstein turned toward me. There was a smile on his face, another sardonic one, I decided. "St. Ives?" he said, making a gesture of offer with the open case.

"No thanks," I said, "I'm trying to give them up."

18

The rental limousine that met us at National Airport in Washington was the twin of the black seven-passenger Cadillac that had taken us to LaGuardia. But there was no similarity in the drivers. The one in New York had been a bitter, snarling Irishman who lectured us on how the niggers were getting all the good jobs until Procane pushed the button that raised the glass divider.

Our Washington driver was a slight, swarthy Cuban with a crisp smile and a high-pitched giggle that he let out each time the traffic went wrong, which it did every thirty seconds or so.

The weather was cold, around thirty degrees, with fat, low clouds that looked as though they wanted to spit wet snow at the Potomac. I had never had any luck with Washington weather. I either froze or fried.

Procane kept looking up at the clouds. He turned to Janet Whistler and said, "Well?"

"It's supposed to clear around five," she said.

I asked Procane why he was so interested.

"If it snows, it's off."

"No snow," the driver said, cheerfully joining the conversation. His name was Manuel Carasa and he had the total unself-consciousness of those who like to strike up conversations at bus stops. "My nose say no snow," he said, pointing to it so that we could be sure where it was. "From the first time I see snow six, seven years ago I can smell it. Always. No snow today."

"What a relief," Janet Whistler said.

"How did you get out of Cuba?" Wiedstein asked the driver.

"Castro, he let me go. First to Miami. Very nice there. Very warm. No snow. I learn English there. Then I come to Washington where it is very beautiful but not so warm except in the summer when it is very warm like Havana. Washington is more beautiful than Havana, no?"

"It's pretty in the spring," Wiedstein said. "I was here in April once with my high school senior class."

"One could paint here," Procane said. "I think it's because of the trees. That should be a beautiful spot in the spring and fall."

We were just past Seventeenth Street going west on Independence Avenue and Procane was looking out at a wooded area just south of the reflecting pool. In the middle of the woods was a small, fake Greek temple. For some reason it didn't seem out of place.

"What's that, driver?" Procane said.

"Memorial to dead in World War Number One," he said. "All dead man's names are written in stone. Just dead from Washington though, not dead from all over."

"It's rather pleasant," Procane said.

127

"Over there at right is Lincoln Memorial," the driver said. "Very famous."

"Thank you," Wiedstein said.

We went past the Lincoln Memorial and then along a four-lane highway that separated the Potomac from the Kennedy Center for the Performing Arts. The Kennedy Center jutted out over the highway as if it wanted to edge as close to the river as it could. It had a series of round gold pipes running up its marble sides, but they looked to me as though they'd been added as an afterthought and a none too inspired one at that.

The center's neighbor was the Watergate cooperative apartment complex where prices started at $44,000 for a one-bedroom unit and shot up to $150,000 for a three-bedroom affair with a wood-burning fireplace and a view of the river. I tried to remember whether I knew anyone who lived there, but decided that I didn't although a future client might turn up in the place someday if the burglary rate continued to fulfill its early promise.

The driver started to snake the Cadillac through a series of switchbacks and crossovers and underneath what seemed to be an elevated highway of some kind. He made a right turn and about three blocks later I knew we were in Georgetown because I recognized the Rive Gauche, a pretty good restaurant where I'd once had some excellent snails.

If Washington has a ghetto, I suppose it's Georgetown. Although anyone can live there, you'd probably feel more comfortable about it if you were rich or white, preferably both. Its narrow streets are lined with some fine old trees and some skinny houses all shouldered up together that are rather old, too, or try to look that way. If you'd bought one when Kennedy came in you could probably sell it now and double your money.

The young also live in Georgetown. The bright, quick, upwardly mobile young, and they give it a false sense of informality. Its real rulers are the rich, quiet, powerful families who eat politics three times a day and hunger for more. The rich and powerful also give Georgetown its hoity-toity air that makes a lot of its residents reluctant to be seen lugging home a six-pack of beer. Not quite forty years ago a large chunk of Georgetown was black slum so there may be hope for Harlem after all.

We turned right on N Street and two or three blocks later the driver stopped in front of a three-story house built of bricks that were painted white. The house was almost flush with the sidewalk as were its neighbors. The houses in that block were jammed up against each other. They were all brick and painted either gray or white and their lines were faintly federal, I think.

"Didn't John Kennedy live on this street when he was a senator?" I said.

"A block or so on down," Procane said and then told the driver to be back at ten that night. He led the way up the seven steps to the small porch, took out a key, and unlocked the door.

"That you, Mistah Procane?" It was a woman's voice calling from somewhere in the rear of the house. He called back that it was and then turned to me. "My housekeeper, Mrs. Williams. She came down from New York yesterday to get the place ready."

A black woman of about fifty-five dressed in a white uniform came into the entrance hall and started collecting our coats. Procane introduced her to me and she said, how do, and started hanging the coats up in a closet.

"How many you gonna be for dinner?" she said.

"Just the four of us," Procane said and led the way into the living room. It had a huge chandelier that must have been a hundred years old because it used real candles instead of electric lights. There was a worn oriental rug on the floor that was probably as old as the chandelier and maybe even more expensive.

The furniture was low with curving, spindly legs and I wondered whether people were that much shorter in the late eighteenth century. On the walls were some oil portraits, darkened by age, and above the mantel was a large mirror with a gilt frame. I didn't see any ashtrays.

The housekeeper followed us into the room and told Procane, "I spect y'all be wantin some coffee," and Procane said yes, coffee would be fine. She nodded and headed back toward the kitchen, going through a formal dining room that was separated from the living room by a set of richly molded sliding doors. There was a long, narrow table of dark burnished wood in the dining room, some chairs that to me looked more frail than delicate, and another chandelier that had to depend on candles.

"Well, Mr. St. Ives, how do you like it?" Procane said.

"Is this the hideout?"

He smiled. "Why, yes, I suppose it could be called that."

"Is it yours?"

He shook his head. "No, I've merely leased it for six months. The lease has two more months to run. I've been coming down here at least once a week for the past four months, usually to give small dinners for several key congressmen and senators. Lobbying really."

"For what?"

"I chose one of the conservation measures. It gave me an excuse for renting the house and I actually became quite interested in this particular bill. Did you realize that we're slaughtering our wildlife at a simply appalling rate?"

"So I've heard."

"I may even have done some good."

"And when you weren't lobbying, you were planning," I said.

"Every detail."

"It's rather elaborate."

"But necessary."

"Wouldn't a motel be just as good?" I said and crossed my legs. The armless chair that I was sitting in creaked. It was upholstered in a worn, mauve-colored fabric that might have been royal purple a hundred years ago. Its back had the shape of a flattened light bulb.

"Not if something goes wrong," Procane said.

"For instance?"

"If the police are brought in. They might check motels. They don't check private residences on N Street."

"You told the driver to be back at ten tonight. That means it's going to happen before ten. Can I ask when?"

"At precisely nine," Procane said.

"Can I ask where?"

Procane seemed to think about that for a moment. "Yes, I think I can tell you that now. At a drive-in movie."

"That's where the buy will take place?"

"Yes."

"Drive-in movies are good," I said. "I've used them three or four times."

"I can see how they would be in your line of work," Procane said. "Moving around at a drive-in movie is nothing unusual. People are always going to the refreshment stand. Cars arrive and depart at any time. It's dark, which offers some concealment. And it's usually fairly crowded, which offers some safety."

The housekeeper came in carrying a tray that held a silver coffee service and four cups and saucers. Procane thanked her and then nodded at Janet Whistler who poured and served the coffee. Nobody wanted cream and no one took any sugar except me.

We sat there in that stiff living room of the house on N Street at four o'clock in the afternoon, drinking coffee like four strangers who had been named to a committee that was supposed to do something that we weren't quite sure that we really wanted done. So we sipped our coffee and talked about how good it was and about the weather and about the room's furnishings and whether antiques were a good investment.

Then we were silent for a while, as if all possible topics had been exhausted, except the one that we had met to talk about but no one wanted to be the one who brought it up. The silence went on for four or five minutes until I said, "What happens to those other guys?"

"What other guys?" Procane said.

"He means the ones who're going to try to steal the million and blame it on us," Wiedstein said.

"I was wondering when you were going to bring them up," Janet Whistler said.

"Now that I have, what happens to them?"

"It depends," Procane said.

"On what?"

"On whether they follow the plan that they stole from me."

"What if they don't?"

Procane shook his head. "If they don't," he said, "I will probably feel quite sorry for them."

19

There were pork chops for dinner, double-cut ones with ruffled white pants so that you wouldn't get your hands greasy when you picked them up and gnawed at the meat close to the bone, which everyone did except Janet Whistler who didn't seem to be too hungry.

There were also mashed potatoes, creamed spinach, and a salad and I ate everything that was set before me, including two pieces of apple pie, not forgetting to compliment Mrs. Williams on her cooking. She shook her head and said, "I don't think that crust was too good."

There hadn't been much conversation at dinner either and there was even less afterward. We had coffee in the living room again. And since there didn't seem to be anything that we wanted to talk about Miles Wiedstein went upstairs and came back down with a small, portable Sony television set. He plugged it in and we listened to Walter Cronkite skim over the news.

When Cronkite said, "And that's the way it is, Wednesday, November the third," Miles Wiedstein turned the set off before Cronkite could tell us what year it was.

"Well," Procane said, rising, "the world seems no worse than usual—nor better either." He looked at his watch. "It's now seven-thirty. We will leave here promptly at eight-twenty. I suggest that we retire for the next forty-five minutes to collect our thoughts and, if possible, relax." He looked at me. "Mr. Wiedstein will show you your room."

"This way," Wiedstein said. I followed him into the hall and up a flight of carpeted stairs. "That one there," he said, pointing to a door. "We share a bath. If you hear me throwing up, don't pay any attention. I always throw up before one of these things."

"Maybe you shouldn't have eaten."

He shook his head. "I like to throw up. It gives me something to do. It doesn't mean I'm sick. Not really sick."

My room had a canopied bed, a bureau, a dresser, two chairs, and a chaise longue. I went through the drawers but they were empty. So was the closet. The

133

two windows were decorated with pale yellow curtains. Their shades were down. I raised one of the shades and saw that I had a view of N Street. It was dark outside. I lowered the shade and stretched out on the bed, staring up at the canopy. I heard some footsteps in the hall. A door closed. Then another one. I shut my eyes and kept them that way, even when I heard my hall door open. I heard movement in the room and someone breathing, but I kept my eyes closed. At the sound of a zipper being unzipped I opened my eyes. It was Janet Whistler and she was half out of her gray pantsuit, the top half. She had nothing on underneath it.

"Move over," she said, stepping out of her pants. I moved over. She eased herself onto the bed next to me and started working on my tie. "You don't have to do anything," she said. "I don't want you to do anything."

"I don't mind doing something," I said, putting an arm around her. "It gives me a sense of participation."

"No," she said, now working on my shirt buttons. "I want it to last."

"I can cooperate along those lines, too. We've got forty minutes or so."

She started unfastening my belt. "That's how long it's got to last. Forty minutes."

"Why?"

"Because it keeps me from thinking. I don't want to think. Not until it really starts."

All of my clothes were off now and we lay on the bed, our arms around each other. I started to say something, to pay her some compliment probably, maybe about how pretty she was, but she shook her head and said, "Don't talk. I don't want to talk. I just want to do everything as though it were the last time ever. For both of us."

She was able to pretend that better than I. There was something frantic about her tongue and hands. Her tongue went exploring, darting into every opening and crevice that she could find. Her nails raked my buttocks and my back again and I had to bite my lip to keep from yelling. But to bite my lip I had to close my mouth and she didn't like that. She wanted it open so that my tongue could be where she thought it should be.

It went like that for what seemed to me a long time although I didn't keep track. And then I was inside her and she began to make small little moans as she writhed and clamped at me and crosshatched my back with her fingernails. "Now hurt me," she said, almost choking on the words, "I want you to hurt me bad." So I hurt her, but not bad, even though she'd wanted me to, and I felt the spasms start in her belly, once, twice, three times, and I quit worrying about her and started delighting in myself and then it started to be over and then it was and we lay there breathing hard and listening to Wiedstein throw up in the bathroom.

"Jesus," I said, turned over, and started fumbling through my clothes for a cigarette.

"He always does that," she said. "I always do this. This is better."

"Who's your usual partner?" I said, offering her a cigarette.

"It depends on where I am. Sometimes it's just me."

"That's not much fun."

"It depends on your imagination. Don't worry, you're not cutting out either Wiedstein or Procane."

"I wasn't worried."

The bathroom door opened and Wiedstein stood there, looking a little pale. I'm not sure that he noticed we were naked. I don't think he cared. He was sponging off his face with a wet cloth.

"You'd better get ready," he said.

"Are you okay now?" Janet Whistler said, propping herself up on one elbow.

"I think it's over. I thought my goddamned appendix was coming up."

"What time is it?" she said.

He looked at his watch. I thought about covering myself with something, but decided that if it wasn't bothering them, it shouldn't bother me. "Eight-ten," he said, turned, and closed the door behind him.

Janet Whistler turned toward me and stretched. "God, I feel better."

"Why don't you go in the bathroom and see if you can find something to put on my back," I said. "I think I'm bleeding all over the counterpane."

"Turn over."

I turned over and she said. "How'd you ever do that?" I think she really didn't know.

I sighed. "It's something like stigmata except that I get it on my back every time I screw."

"You mean I did that?"

"Didn't anyone ever complain before?"

"No. Never. Really they didn't."

"Am I bleeding?"

"Not really. They're just scratches, but I'll put something on them."

"Don't bother," I said, swinging my legs over the bed and reaching for my shirt.

"Did I do that before?" she asked. "I mean when we were up at your place?"

"Yes."

"I never did it to anyone else. Honestly."

"Maybe they were too polite to complain."

"They weren't that polite. Nobody is."

"Forget it."

"I think I know why I do it."

"Why?"

"It's like I told you before. You're such a good fuck. But you know what you can do next time?"

"What?"

"You can buy me some gloves."

Mrs. Williams fetched our coats from the hall closet and we shrugged into them in the living room and then stood around, a little awkwardly, like guests at a party that has lasted too long.

Procane turned to Mrs. Williams and said, "The car will be by for you at ten."

"Yes, sir."

"I'll be back in New York some time tomorrow."

"In time for lunch or dinner?"

"Dinner, I think."

"Yes, sir."

"Thank you for coming down, Mrs. Williams, and for the fine dinner."

"You welcome, Mr. Procane."

He turned to us then and said, "We can go out through the back."

We followed him through the dining room, a pantry, and the kitchen that had one of those large, commercial stoves that can cook for four or forty. There was also a big freezer, an outsized refrigerator, and two automatic dishwashers.

"They entertain a lot," Procane said, apparently referring to the absent owners of the house. He opened a door that led outside and we went down a flight of wooden steps from a small porch into a back yard. Procane had switched on an outside light and I could see that the term *back yard* wasn't quite grand enough for the small, carefully laid out informal garden that had cost somebody a great deal of money and even more time. It was too dark to recognize the shrubs and bushes, and I'm not sure that I could have anyhow, but some of them were cozily wrapped up in burlap against the winter frost. There were five or six tall shade trees, nearly bare now, and curving in and out of the shrubs and the trees was a walk of white gravel that sparkled in the artificial light.

We followed the walk until we came to a brick garage. Procane used a key to unlock a door and we went inside. He turned on another light and it revealed two three- or four-year-old Chevrolet Impalas. One was black and the other was green. There was still space enough in the garage for a third car, a big one such as a Cadillac or an Imperial. There was even enough space for the long workbench that ran along one side of the garage and which had enough tools to put a shade-tree mechanic in business.

Procane moved over, inserted another key in a wall lock of some kind, pushed a button, and the garage's overhead door rose smoothly. "We'll take the green one, Mr. St. Ives," he said and motioned for me to get in. He went around to the driver's side. Wiedstein and Janet Whistler got in the black car, Wiedstein at the wheel.

Procane waited until Wiedstein backed out of the garage and started up the alley. Then he started our engine and we followed, turning left and then right on N Street and then left on Wisconsin Avenue and right again on M Street, which, along with Wisconsin, is one of the two main drags through Georgetown.

Wiedstein stayed in the left lane. He signaled for a left turn just before we got to Key Bridge, but had to wait for a red light. We waited, just behind him.

"What's it going to be," I said, "Maryland or Virginia?"

"Virginia," Procane said. "Do you have a preference?"

"No."

"Have you been in Virginia before?"

"I stopped at Bull Run once."

"Was it interesting?"

"Sort of."

The light turned green and we crossed the Potomac over the bridge that was named after the composer of our national anthem who, I've always suspected, had a tin ear. At the Virginia side of Key Bridge we turned right and about half a mile later edged on to the George Washington Memorial Parkway.

"No last-minute instructions?" I said. "Not even a pep talk?"

"They really don't need it," Procane said, holding the Impala to a steady fifty miles per hour about five car lengths behind Wiedstein.

"They seemed a little nervous to me," I said.

"Of course they are, aren't you?"

"No, I'm just scared."

Procane chuckled. "I can't decide whether what I feel is apprehension or anticipation. Perhaps a little of both. Whatever it is, I like it. I really do."

"Maybe you're just a born thief."

Procane chuckled again. "Maybe I am at that."

We drove for nearly fifteen minutes until we came to a fork in the parkway. To the right lay Maryland; to the left, Virginia. We went left down a two-lane, one-way road that hooked sharply left again. The rear stop-lights on Wiedstein's car flashed on as he slowed down.

"The beltway," Procane said. "U.S. 495. It goes all the way around Washington."

It was a six-lane highway, three lanes on each side, and a sign I spotted put the speed limit at sixty-five, but nobody but Procane and Wiedstein seemed to observe it. Cars flicked by us going at least eighty or even ninety. The traffic was moderate for that time of night.

Procane drove well and I was a little surprised because not too many New Yorkers do, probably because not many of them own cars. The last car I had owned had been when I'd lived in Chicago, nearly fourteen years ago. It had been a Studebaker. They don't make them like that anymore and I can understand why.

"I'm really surprised, Mr. St. Ives," Procane said.

"At what?"

"That you didn't back out. I thought you might have second thoughts."

"I did."

"But here you are."

"Yes, here I am."

"What you're doing is really quite criminal, you know."

"I suppose it is."

"That doesn't bother you?"

"Not much. Maybe because my values are twisted."

"You mean stealing a million dollars from drug merchants is quite different from stealing a million dollars from—say—a bank?"

"That's what I keep telling myself."

"Do you believe it?"

"Part of it."

"Which part?"

"About the drug dealers," I said. "It'll hurt them. Not much, but some. I don't want to be preachy and all that good shit, but heroin's nasty stuff. It wrecks too many lives and the people whose lives it wrecks are usually those who have everything going against them anyway."

"And that's what you've used to justify your coming along?"

"It doesn't justify it, but it helps explain it. I tell myself that there's something redeeming about what I'm doing. Not much maybe, but something."

"Of course, it might just increase the price of heroin. That means that the addicts will have to steal more to feed their habits. More crime will result. If the addicts resort to armed robbery, some innocent persons may get killed. Have you thought about it in that light?"

"No."

"It's better not to."

"How do you think about it?"

"I accept what I am first. I'm a thief. But I steal only from those who've done something illegal. That way I salve my conscience." He paused. "If I have one." He seemed to brood about that for a few moments and then said, "Tell me something."

"What?"

"When was the last time you stole something?"

"What makes you sure there was a last time?"

Procane chuckled again. "Don't fence with me. When was it?"

"Not counting the pencils I used to take home from the office?"

"Not counting those."

"It was 1944 in Columbus, Ohio."

"You were a child."

"That's right."

"What did you steal?"

"A magazine from a drugstore."

"Why?"

"Because I wanted it and I didn't have a dime."

"How bad did you want it?"

I thought about that. "I think I wanted it more than anything I ever wanted in my life."

"And after you stole it how did you feel?"

"Scared. Remorseful. Guilt-ridden."

"Did you enjoy the magazine?"

"No."

Once more Procane chuckled, this time deep down in his throat as if he really found something funny. "I'll tell you one thing about yourself, Mr. St. Ives."

"What?"

"You'll never make a proper thief."

"Why, because stealing makes me feel guilty?"

"No, you could probably live with that. It's something else."

"What?"

"You don't really like it. To be a good thief you've got to really enjoy your work."

I remember thinking that that was the first time I'd ever heard Procane split an infinitive, but I decided that he'd probably done it on purpose.

20

We traveled the beltway for five or six miles and then turned off at Exit 17 on to State Highway 27 which turned out to be a narrow, winding two-lane asphalt road that traveled west.

Ahead of us Wiedstein cut his speed to forty-five miles per hour and we kept our five-car-lengths' distance. I couldn't see much of the countryside. A few lighted houses far back from the road. Some trees. An occasional bridge across a creek—or run, as they are called in Virginia. A gas station or two. Several hand-lettered signs along the road advertising "Puppies for Sale."

I found myself wishing that Mrs. Williams had served carrots for dinner. They might have helped my night vision. When I was through thinking about that I thought about how I came to be riding down a Virginia highway, driven by a master thief, following a couple of his apprentices who were about to turn journeymen, and headed for a million-dollar robbery that was going to make some very unpleasant people extremely unhappy.

But it wasn't going to be a simple gun-in-the-ribs heist. It was going to be something tricky because there were some others who wanted to steal the million dollars. Not only did these others want to steal it, but they also had a blueprint—stolen from the master thief himself—that told them just how to go about it. And when it was over, they could blame it all on him.

I wondered who the others were and what plans

Procane had for them, but because there was no sense in either wondering or asking about that, I started thinking about Bright Bobby Boykins, a small-time con artist who had aspired to better things and had been beaten to death just for trying. I remember how Boykins had looked, trussed up and tucked away out of sight behind the laundromat's dryers. Then I remembered how Jimmy Peskoe had looked after he had hit the sidewalk in front of a cheap hotel, his safe-cracking days over and whatever knowledge he had about Procane's journals and what they contained now safely buried.

And finally I remembered the pride of the motor-scooter patrol, Francis X. Frann, who had wanted to be a plainclothes detective—or to shake down Procane—or both. I decided he had picked the wrong case and I remembered how still he had sat behind the wheel of the car, the shoulder harness holding him upright, the fatal stab wound not even showing.

Frann had known those who had had the Procane journals and whoever it was probably had killed him, just as they had killed Boykins and Peskoe.

If they had killed three, it wouldn't matter much to them (for some reason I thought of the killer or killers as them) if they killed two more, or three, or even half a dozen. A million dollars in cash is a lot of money and many have killed more for much less.

As I thought about the three persons who had died during the past four days there was something about each death that began to bother me. There seemed to be a link and I thought I almost had it when Procane said, "We're nearly there."

The drive-in movie was on the left-hand side of the road. A red-neon sign said that it was called The Big Ben Drive-In, possibly because of the rhyme. Below the neon sign was the lighted marquee which boasted of presenting a "Triple XXX Feature!" The names of the films were *Take Me Naked, The Daisy Chain*, and *Unsatisfied*.

143

I looked at my watch and it was ten minutes till nine.

"We're a little early," Procane said.

"I'd hate to miss the beginning."

"We won't."

He slowed down and made the turn into the drive-in.

Wiedstein was already at the enclosed ticket booth, handing some money through his car window to a middle-aged woman. Procane drove slowly, letting Wiedstein get past the booth before we stopped.

Procane rolled down his window. "How much?"

"Three bucks each," the woman said. She was bundled in a navy pea coat whose collar came up around the frizzled gray hair that framed her chapped face. A cigarette dangled from her lips. I couldn't tell whether the twist in her upper lip was because of the smoke or whether it was a sneer that advised her customers of how she felt about them.

Procane handed her a ten and she dug a small roll out of her pea coat and stripped off four ones. "If you hurry," she said, handing him the money, "you'll catch the beginning of *Daisy Chain*."

Procane put a lisp and a lilt in his tone. "We wouldn't want to miss that, would we?"

"I simply couldn't bear it," I said.

"Fuckin fags," the woman said and slid the booth's glass window shut.

The entrance road of the drive-in was lined by high board fences. The fence on the left ended after about fifteen yards but the one on the right continued all around the drive-in—to keep out the nonpaying customers, I assumed.

The screen was near the highway and the parking spaces with their individual speakers and heaters fanned out from it. In the middle of the parking space was a low, cinder-block building that housed the projection booth and the refreshment stand. As Procane drove slowly along the fence with his lights off I counted about three dozen cars. Business was slow.

At the very back row Procane drove the car up the slight parking incline and stopped.

"Where's Wiedstein and the girl?" I said.

"The next row up and to your right."

"I don't see them in the car."

"They've gone for refreshments."

"Where am I supposed to be looking so that I can record all this for posterity?"

"The third row up."

"There's nothing there."

"There will be."

"When?"

Procane looked at his watch. "You've got about five minutes. Relax and enjoy the show."

I looked at the screen. A woman was helping another woman take off her brassiere. Neither of them was very pretty. When the brassiere was off, a man came into what seemed to be a bedroom. The woman who was having her brassiere removed looked embarrassed and tried to cover her breasts. The other woman grinned. So did the man and then they started talking to each other and I stopped looking.

"You'd better bring the speaker inside," Procane said.

"Okay." I rolled down the window, took the speaker out of its wire holder, and fitted it over the edge of the window which I rolled back up.

"You want it on?" I said.

"Not unless you do."

"No, thanks."

Procane looked at his watch again. "In about thirty seconds a blue Dodge convertible should be arriving and parking three rows up and to our left."

"Now many in it?"

"One."

"The South American?"

"Right."

We waited thirty seconds, but nothing happened.

"He's late," I said.

"You're nervous."

"You're right."

Fifteen seconds or so later a blue Dodge convertible with a white top crept down the third row. The driver's face was a pale blur. The car turned up the slight incline and parked. The driver didn't bother to bring the speaker inside.

I saw Wiedstein and Janet Whistler approaching their car. Wiedstein carried a cardboard tray. It looked as though he had a bag of popcorn and two Cokes, but I couldn't be sure at that distance. They got in the car and then melted together, apparently in an embrace. Or clinch.

"Neckers?" I said.

"That's right."

"It's a pretty good place for it."

"I can't think of a better."

"What are we waiting for now?"

"A car with four men in it."

"What kind of car?"

"I don't know."

It was a dark-colored Oldsmobile, a big sedan, either blue or black. It rolled down the third row and then parked next to the Dodge convertible. The stand that held the two speakers separated them. There were four men in the car. They didn't bother with a speaker either.

"Look to your left and up four rows," Procane said. "See those two men?"

"The ones who're carrying something?"

"They're coming from the refreshment stand."

"What about them?"

"'They're the ones who're going to steal the million dollars."

I didn't ask him how he knew. I stared at the two men. It was still too far away to see their faces. They wore topcoats and hats. The hats were pulled down low. They were moving toward my left, walking slowly, carrying a tray each. I looked to the left. There were no cars parked there. The two men were now near the left-front fender of the Dodge convertible, the car that contained the South American diplomat.

Both of the men raised their right hands to their faces.

"Stocking masks," Procane whispered. "They're following it exactly."

With an abrupt motion they threw away their refreshment trays. The first man, a little taller than the other, leaped forward and grabbed the handle of the Dodge door, jerking it open. The second man leaned inside the car for no more than three seconds. I expected to hear a shot, but I heard nothing.

"Mace," Procane said. "They maced him."

They left the Dodge's door open and ran quickly around its rear. The first man headed for the far right side of the Oldsmobile. The second man darted toward the rear left side. The four doors of the sedan flew open simultaneously. Someone seemed to make a lunge out of the rear seat. I rolled my window down. There was a shout and the figure that had lunged out of the car crumpled to the ground. He rolled about.

"More Mace?" I said.

"Yes."

The man on the left side of the Oldsmobile now leaned forward into the front seat of the car. Then he straightened up and leaned into the rear. When he came out he was carrying something that looked like a one-suiter. The man on the right side of the Oldsmobile now hurried around its rear. Both men trotted to the Dodge. One of them, the shorter one, bent forward inside the car. I could no longer see its occupant. He was probably writhing around on the front seat, clawing at his eyes. When the man who was leaning into the Dodge straightened up I could see that he was carrying something in his right hand. It looked like a suitcase, a heavy one. He handed it to the man who already was carrying the suitcase that he had taken from the Oldsmobile. He sagged under the weight of both cases. He should have if they contained what I thought they did.

The man who had lifted the suitcase out of the Dodge now lifted out another one. It looked heavy, too. The two men, carrying the three cases, began to run. There were shouts and groans from the Oldsmobile now. A man staggered out from its front seat, spun around, and sank to his knees. His hands were at his face. It looked a little as if he were praying. He may have been.

The two men with the three suitcases were running toward the refreshment stand. They didn't run very fast, not with what they were carrying.

"They took the heroin," Procane said. He sounded surprised.

"About one hundred and ten pounds' worth, I'd say. Wasn't it part of your plan?"

He started the engine. "No, that wasn't in my plan."

"Now what?"

"Put the speaker back and watch Wiedstein."

I watched Wiedstein. He was no longer in the clinch with Janet Whistler. He was backing his car out savagely. The rear wheels chewed up the gravel as he slammed into drive and gunned forward, heading for the exit.

I watched Wiedstein's car as it streaked toward the narrow exit that was lined by two high board fences. The exit road curved on its way back to the highway and I lost sight of Wiedstein's car.

"Now what?" I said again.

"We back out like this," Procane said and reversed the car sedately until we were headed toward the exit. "Now we wait another moment or two."

A small green Mustang with its lights off came out from behind the refreshment stand and sped toward the exit. Procane glanced at his watch and then put his car in drive and headed toward the exit. His speed was barely above normal.

"They didn't do too badly, everything considered," he said.

"I thought they looked like pros."

"Well, they were a little off."

"How?"

"I had it timed for forty-five seconds. It took them nearly fifty-five."

I looked back at the Dodge and the Oldsmobile. I could see three or four men weaving around. They all seemed to have handkerchiefs to their eyes. "How long will that bunch be out of action?"

"Oh, several minutes more. Perhaps even longer. That Mace is very tricky stuff."

"So I've heard," I said and then asked, "What now?" for the third time.

"Now? Now we steal a million dollars from a couple of thieves."

21

It was a trap. I could see it when Procane rounded the curve of the narrow, fence-bordered exit road. About thirty feet from where the fences ended, Wiedstein had blocked the road by angling his car across the narrow strip of asphalt. The hood was up. I could see neither Wiedstein nor Janet Whistler.

The green Mustang was just skidding to a stop when we came around the curve. Its taillights glared at us for what seemed to be a long time before the car stopped some ten feet from Wiedstein's Chevrolet. I rolled my window down. So did Procane who kept on driving slowly toward the stopped Mustang.

The doors of the Mustang flew open. A man got out on the right side. I could see the gloss of the nylon stocking that covered the back of his head beneath the brim of his hat. He yelled something. It sounded like, "Move that fuckin thing!"

Wiedstein came out from behind the raised hood of his car. He was fully illuminated by the Mustang's headlights. He spread his hands in a gesture that seemed to say, The damned thing stopped on me and I can't get it started. The man with the stocking mask ducked back into the Mustang and when he reappeared he was holding something in his hands. It was a sawed-off pump shotgun.

Procane switched on our bright lights. The man looked back at us, called something to the Mustang's driver, and started walking toward Wiedstein's stalled car. The driver of the Mustang got out and turned toward us. He waved something. It was a gun, an automatic.

"Brace yourself!" Procane snapped. He pressed down on the accelerator. I grabbed for the padded dash. We slammed into the rear of the Mustang at about fifteen miles per hour. It made a sickening, grinding kind of a crunch and crash, the kind that you know is going to cost at least four hundred dollars.

The Mustang bounced forward, but not much. It must have been in park gear. The man with the automatic pistol staggered back a step, but recovered quickly. He used his left hand to shield his eyes against the glare of our left headlight. Procane hadn't hit the Mustang's rear squarely. The man with the pistol fired. The gun flash and the cobwebbed hole in our windshield seemed to happen at the same time.

"Out on your side!" Procane said, barking the words.

I opened the door and tumbled out onto the asphalt,

skinning my left knee. Procane followed. We knelt behind the car and its open door.

"Close it," Procane said.

I slammed the door shut.

"Not much of a view from here," I said.

"Just imagine it," Procane said. He had his engraved automatic in his right hand now. He knelt next to me, trying to peer around the Mustang we'd slammed into as though he wanted to see what Wiedstein and Janet Whistler were doing.

We heard three shots. They weren't rapid fire, but as if someone were squeezing them off carefully, counting by thousands between each pull of the trigger.

The man with the sawed-off shotgun darted out from in front of the Mustang and ran toward the right side of Wiedstein's car. He was bent over low, trying to scuttle toward the upraised hood at the front of the car. I decided that the carefully spaced shots had been covering fire.

"Hold it right there!" Procane yelled at the man with the shotgun. I thought there was a lot of authority in Procane's tone. So did the man with the shotgun, because he twirled around. If he'd have pulled the trigger a fraction of a second later, he would have cut us in two.

The man with the shotgun was about twenty feet from us. Procane fired at him, but missed. I had started backing toward the rear of the car. Procane fired again, but again missed. I decided that he was a lousy shot.

The man with the shotgun seemed to smile. At least I thought I saw something white through his stocking mask. He raised the shotgun to his shoulder. I was still backing crablike toward the rear of the car. Procane got off another shot, but I didn't expect him to hit anything. He didn't. The man with the shotgun was aiming it now. He couldn't miss Procane. If he did, he'd hit me. Procane started backing up.

151

Janet Whistler stepped out from behind the raised hood of Wiedstein's car and killed the man with the shotgun by shooting him in the back three times.

His head jerked back like in whiplash and his hands flew out at the first shot. The shotgun sailed off somewhere. He took a small, mincing step toward us and when the second bullet hit him he twitched a little, almost as if it were the second step of some new and elaborate dance. He was beginning to fall when the third bullet hit him and hammered him to the ground. He fell toward us, full length, like a toppled tree. He didn't use his hands to break his fall. He twitched once, then twice, but after that he didn't twitch anymore.

"I'm a rotten shot," Procane said.

"I agree."

Janet Whistler looked at the dead man for a moment. She stood quite still, her arms at her side, the automatic almost dangling from her right hand. Then she turned and disappeared behind the front of Wiedstein's car.

"This way," Procane said. He bent over, almost double, and started to move slowly around the rear of his car. I followed him, not because I thought that he was much protection, but because I didn't want to be alone.

When we were on the other side of Procane's car we started edging toward the Mustang. Its left door was open. The left headlight of Procane's car was still on bright and it bathed that side of the Mustang in harsh yellow light.

When we had crept almost even with the front wheels of the Chevrolet, Procane called, "There're four of us and we're armed. Your partner's dead. You'd better give up."

We waited, but there was no reply. Procane rose. I was next to him now and I rose too. Slowly.

"Put your hands on your head and step out where we can see you," Procane called. I glanced at him. His eyes sparkled and there was a tight grin beneath his ginger moustache. The moustache fairly bristled. Procane seemed to be enjoying his work.

The man stepped out from behind the Mustang's open door into the glare of our single headlight, but his hands weren't on top of his head. Instead the right one was wrapped around the grip of his automatic and the left one was bracing his right wrist. He was in a half-crouch. It was a thoroughly professional stance, the kind that expert pistol shooters go into when they want to make sure that they'll hit what they're aiming at. The automatic pistol was aimed right at me.

It all fell into place then, of course, just as I was about to die. It was partly intuitive leap, but mostly it was remembering small things that happened when they shouldn't have happened. If I hadn't been going to die so soon, I could have told someone all about my wonderful memory and the brilliant deductive process that was my mind. I could also have told them who killed Bobby Boykins and who threw Jimmy Peskoe out of an eighth-story window.

Procane tried, of course. He pulled the trigger of his Walther, the one with all the fancy engraving on its slide. Something made a dry little click that had a disparaging sound to it, like the "tch-tch" you make with your teeth and tongue when something that's of minor importance goes wrong.

I was going to die, of course, and I didn't think that that was anything minor, but there was nothing I could do about it except stare at the gun that was leveled at me with rock-steady aim. I was just beginning to wonder about why he didn't go ahead and get it over with when a man's voice called, "Behind you, friend!"

The man whirled, still in his gunfighter's crouch. He was nearly all the way around before the first bullet smashed into him. He fired back, but his aim was off and I don't think he even came close to Miles Wiedstein who walked toward him now, firing as he came. Wiedstein shot the man in the stocking mask three times before he hit the ground. The first shot seemed to double him over, the second one straightened him up, and the third sent him staggering backward toward Procane and me.

He fell before he reached us. His arms were flung out carelessly at his sides. His unbuttoned jacket and topcoat gaped open. I could have placed a small saucer over the three red-black holes in the white shirt that gleamed up at the sky. I wondered who had taught Wiedstein how to shoot; it couldn't have been Procane.

Procane turned to me, his eyes fixed on the Walther that he held gingerly in his right hand as if it were some kind of a rare bug. "It misfired," he said.

"So I noticed."

"Yes. I imagine you did. I suppose I should have thrown it at him."

"It doesn't matter now."

He looked at the dead man. "No, it doesn't, does it?"

Wiedstein came up to us followed by Janet Whistler. I thought both of them looked pale and then I wondered how I looked to them.

"He was pretty good," Wiedstein said, touching the dead man's shoulder with his toe."

"Both of them were," Procane said.

"They weren't supposed to be that good," Wiedstein said. "Maybe we'd better find out who they were." He looked at Procane.

Procane started to kneel by the dead man to take off the stocking mask. Janet Whistler turned away. Wiedstein decided to look up at the sky to see what the clouds were like.

"You don't have to do that," I said to Procane.

He looked up at me. "Why?"

"I know who they are," I said and tried not to make my voice sound smug. I think I succeeded because I didn't feel smug.

"Who?"

"That one's Frank Deal. The one with the shotgun was Carl Oller."

"The detectives," Procane said. "They talked to me. Yesterday." He didn't sound as though he believed me.

"All right," I said. "Go ahead. Take it off his face."

Procane grimaced but peeled the stocking from the dead man's face. Frank Deal's cold gray eyes were open. They seemed to be staring at me.

"You want to take a look at the other one?" I said.

"No," Procane said. "That won't be necessary."

He rose and brushed his hands together as though they were covered with dirt. "Why did they do it?" he said, but not as if he expected an answer.

"Two reasons," I said.

"What?"

"The first was a million dollars."

"What was the second one?"

"Today is Wednesday."

"So?"

"Wednesday was their day off."

22

I helped get the three suitcases out of the Mustang's back seat. We put them in the trunk of Wiedstein's car. The one that I carried didn't weigh much, not more than thirty pounds, so I assumed that it was the million dollars in currency. It can weigh far less than a million dollars in heroin.

"What're you going to do with it?" I said as I got in the back seat next to Janet Whistler.

Procane turned to look at me. "With what?"

"The heroin."

"Destroy it, of course. I'm not quite sure—"

He didn't finish his sentence because Wiedstein, not quite into the driver's seat, looked back and said, "Down!"

I turned instead and saw the dark Oldsmobile slide to a stop just behind Procane's car which was still smashed into the Mustang. The four doors of the Oldsmobile again flew open and four men tumbled out. They did some gesturing and some pointing and when they were through with that they seemed to start aiming something in our direction and I lost interest and ducked down behind the rear seat.

Wiedstein had the car moving by the time I heard the first shots. Janet Whistler was also half-lying on the rear seat, her face no more than six inches from mine, her eyes closed. When we felt Wiedstein skid the car onto Highway 27 she opened her eyes and looked at me. Then she smiled and winked. We sat up.

Procane was looking back toward the drive-in's exit. "They're going to try to come out the entrance," he said.

Wiedstein nodded. "I know. I thought Mace was supposed to last longer."

"It does when properly applied."

"They looked awfully unhappy."

"Yes, they did, didn't they? Can you lose them?"

Wiedstein shook his head. "I don't think so."

By now we were just past the entrance to the drive-in and it felt as though we were already hitting eighty miles per hour.

Procane looked back. "They're coming out of the entrance now. Are you sure you can't lose them?"

"I don't know these roads," Wiedstein said. "I might turn down a dead end."

Procane nodded. "Then we'll have to use your alternative method, won't we?"

"Yes," Wiedstein said, "I suppose we will."

I started to ask what the alternative method was and how many persons it might kill and whether I might be among them, but Procane had his own questions and he had to shout them because the speedometer said that we were now doing close to ninety. That was far too fast on that road at night. It was really too fast in daytime. My answers to Procane's shouted questions were almost mechanically shouted replies because I kept watching the road—not only in front of us, but also behind us where the two headlights of the pursuing Oldsmobile crept steadily nearer.

What Procane wanted to know first was, "How did you know—that those two men—were Deal and Oller?" He shouted it above the wind noise in phrases because he kept running out of breath.

"They had to be," I yelled back.

"Why?"

"Little things."

"What little things?"

"At the laundromat."

"What?"

"It was too much of a coincidence."

"How?"

"That they just happened to drop by—right after I found Boykins's body."

Procane shook his head. "That could happen."

"There was something else."

"What?"

"They knew where the body was."

"So?"

"They shouldn't have known because it was hidden. Out of sight. Behind the last dryer. Deal went right to it."

"That didn't worry you then?"

I shook my head. "I didn't think about it then."

"Is that all?"

"No."

"Well?"

"That second phone call you got. The one that set up the switch in the airline terminal."

"What about it?"

Before I could answer Wiedstein twisted around for a brief second. "Put those seat belts on," he shouted.

Janet Whistler and I buckled the belts. Procane drew the front seat's harness belt across his chest. He couldn't turn around now so he shouted his questions at the windshield.

"What about that phone call?"

I turned to look out the rear window before answering. The Oldsmobile seemed closer. Much closer.

"It was the airline bag," I yelled back at him.

"Well?"

"He told me to use that 'same Pan-Am bag.'"

"Ah."

"So how'd he know it was a Pan-Am bag?" I said, still shouting. "He must have seen it. All right. Who had seen the bag? Just the two detectives, Deal and Oller. And the kid cop, Frann."

"And that's all?"

"Some other cops saw it—at the precinct, but they didn't count. Neither did Myron Greene. He saw it, too."

"And the motor-scooter patrolman Frann. He recognized them in the airline terminal?"

"That's right."

"So when you told them that he had, they killed him."

"No."

Procane tried to twist around in his seat. When he couldn't because of the harness belt, he unsnapped it and turned around. "They didn't kill Frann?"

"They couldn't have," I said.

"Why?"

"Because right after I found Frann dead I called Deal. He was home. Oller was with him. He lived in Brooklyn. Frann hadn't been dead that long, not long enough for Deal and Oller to make it to Brooklyn."

"They both had a motive."

"Maybe. But I think they would have tried to cut Frann in for a share rather than kill him."

"All right, who did kill Frann?"

"I don't know. Did you?"

Procane stared at me, a little surprised, I thought. Finally he said, "No. I didn't kill him."

"You had a motive so I thought I'd ask."

"Well, I didn't kill him."

"Then I don't know who did."

"What about the safecracker?"

"Peskoe?"

"Yes."

"They killed him," I said.

"Oller and Deal."

"Yes."

"Another hunch?"

"Not really."

"What?"

"The room clerk at the hotel where Peskoe lived."

"What about him?"

"He told me that just before Peskoe died he saw two men go up in the elevator."

"Oller and Deal?"

I shook my head. "He wasn't sure. He didn't even remember what they looked like. But he did remember one thing."

"What?"

"He never saw them come back down."

"So?"

"So after Peskoe died there were a lot of homicide cops around the hotel. Oller and Deal could have thrown Peskoe out of room eight-nineteen, gone up to the roof, and then come back down and mingled with the other cops when they got there. It was perfect camouflage. It might not have been their case, but nobody was going to ask them why they were there. Homicide was their business. That's why the hotel clerk never saw them again. When they went up, they were just two men he didn't pay much attention to. Whey they came back down, they were cops. In his mind they couldn't be the same."

"Put that belt back on," Wiedstein told Procane.

"Yes, of course," Procane said and turned back around. "That's an interesting theory you have, Mr. St. Ives."

"It's not anything more than that," I said, peering over Wiedstein's shoulder at the speedometer.

"How fast?" Janet Whistler asked.

"It says ninety-five." I twisted around again and saw that the lights of the Oldsmobile were still gaining on us.

"Soon?" Procane asked Wiedstein.

Wiedstein nodded. "I remember a place up here after a series of curves, but we'll have to gain on the curves."

Wiedstein was good, very good. Although he braked sharply, I still thought we had gone into the first curve far too fast because I felt the rear end start to go. Wiedstein felt it, too, and at just the right moment tromped on the accelerator so that the Chevrolet's rear wheels bit into the asphalt and hurtled us forward.

I still don't know how he judged those curves. Not at night at that speed. There were four of them and the warning signs along the road said that none of them should be taken faster than forty-five. In daylight. Just before he went into them Wiedstein was hitting eighty. At night. He would brake to sixty-five and come out of them doing at least eighty-five. It could have been luck, but I preferred to think of it as skill.

On the last curve, a treacherous S-shaped affair, I thought he'd lost his touch. We started a skid that the rear wheels couldn't dig us out of, but Wiedstein steered with the skid for a moment, and then we were racing straight ahead again, but with the lights off.

"What happened to the lights?" I said.

"He turned them off," Procane said.

"Why?"

"He doesn't have time to explain. You'll see in a moment."

It took a little while for my eyes to adjust to the darkness. When they did I could barely make out the road and its white dividing strip. The clouds had disappeared, just as Janet Whistler had promised, and there was part of a cold moon. From its pale light I could see that the road ahead was straight.

I looked behind us. The Oldsmobile was still fighting the curves and no longer in sight. I looked ahead again just in time to see the approaching intersection. Wiedstein slammed on his brakes and at the same time mashed the accelerator all the way to the floor. He spun the steering wheel sharply to the left, let up on the brake, caught some loose gravel at the intersection with his rear wheels, and in less than a second had completed a classic example of what some folks refer to as the bootleggers' racing turn.

We had spun around and now we were speeding right back where we had just been. The lights were still off. Wiedstein had the Chevrolet straddling the center white line. We were doing at least eighty-five by the time the Oldsmobile came out of the last of the curves.

I don't think the driver of the Oldsmobile saw us until Wiedstein flicked on our lights. The bright ones. We were less than two hundred feet from the Oldsmobile then and on its side of the road and the two of us were traveling at a combined speed of around one hundred fifty-five miles per hour.

So the driver of the Oldsmobile had a bare second to decide between the certain death of a head-on crash and the uncertainty of going off the road. He decided to go off the road. He had to go through a guard rail to do it, but he crashed through that without too much trouble. Beyond the guard rail was a gully that was at least ten feet deep and twenty feet wide. It had a fairly gentle slope to it and I watched the Oldsmobile plunge down the slope, turn end over end, and then roll halfway up its farther side before it came to a stop. No doors burst open this time.

"Did it burn?" Wiedstein said.

"I don't think so," I said.

"We'll go back another way," Wiedstein said.

We eventually took Route 7 to the beltway and the George Washington Memorial Parkway to the District of Columbia line. None of us said anything until we turned right off Key Bridge into Georgetown. Then Procane looked at his watch and said, "It's ten past ten. We're right on schedule."

He unfastened his chest harness and turned around in the seat toward me. "Well, Mr. St. Ives, how did you enjoy our million-dollar theft?"

"It was swell," I said. "We'll have to do it again sometime."

23

Wiedstein double-parked the car in front of the house on N Street. Everyone got out. Wiedstein moved back to the trunk and unlocked it and lifted out the three suitcases. Procane picked up two of them and turned to me.

"Will you give me a hand, Mr. St. Ives?"

"Sure," I said and picked up the other one.

Carrying his two suitcases Procane turned toward Wiedstein. "Get rid of the car," he said.

Wiedstein nodded. "I'll leave it some place with the keys in it. Somebody'll steal it."

"I'll be back in New York tomorrow around noon."

"We'll see you then," Janet Whistler said.

My suitcase was growing heavy. I wished that they would end their conversation so that I could carry the suitcase to wherever it was supposed to be carried. It was a new case, I noticed, a two-suiter made out of cloth fiber and trimmed with a plastic that was supposed to look like blue leather, but didn't.

"Is there anything else you can think of, Miles?" Procane said.

Wiedstein said he couldn't think of anything.

"Janet?"

She shook her head.

"Mr. St. Ives?"

"This suitcase is getting heavy."

"Yes, well, I'll see you two tomorrow."

They nodded at him and we stood there on the sidewalk and watched them get in the Chevrolet and drive off down N Street.

I followed Procane up the short flight of steps that led to the door. He had to put one case down so that he could find his keys. As he was fumbling the key into the lock, he said, "You're welcome to spend the night here, Mr. St. Ives, if you'd like."

"I'll decide after I have a drink," I said. "I may want to go back to New York."

"Whichever you prefer."

Procane had the door open now. He went inside, switching on the hall light. I followed. Procane turned on a lamp in the living room. It all looked much the same as it had nearly two hours before except for the man who sat in one of the spindly-legged chairs and pointed the revolver at us.

I guessed that the man was in his late forties. His legs looked long enough to make him well over six feet tall, but it may have been because of the way he had them stretched out in front of him and crossed at the ankles. It was a casual pose, but there was nothing casual about the way he aimed the revolver at us. It had a long barrel and I thought that it looked like a .38

163

caliber. The man moved the barrel from side to side a little, as if he couldn't make up his mind about which of us he wanted to shoot first.

"You can put that away, John," Procane said. "There's no need for it now."

"Set the bags down, Abner," John said. "You, too, St. Ives."

I still didn't know who he was, but I put the bag down anyway. When the bags were safely on the floor, the man said, "Now both of your put your hands on top of your heads." I did just what he wanted. Procane didn't. Instead, he said, "This is ridiculous."

"Put your hands up there, Abner," the man said. This time Procane did as he was told.

I turned my head slowly toward Procane. "Who's John?" I said.

"John Constable."

"Ah," I said, "the analyst."

"That's right, St. Ives," Constable said, "the analyst."

I ignored him. "He's the one you always talked to about your problems," I said to Procane. "About whether you wanted to get caught."

Procane just nodded. His face had grown pink. I didn't know whether it was embarrassment or anger.

"You told him all about tonight," I said, not making it a question because there was no need to.

"I told him all about it," Procane said.

"Is it becoming clear, St. Ives?" Constable said, rising from his chair. He wasn't quite as tall as I'd thought, just barely six feet. But his legs were still long, too long really for his short trunk, and it made him look bird-legged. He tried to cover it up with a carefully tailored, extra-long jacket, but it didn't quite come off. He still looked bird-legged. His jacket was cut from a soft-brown plaid that looked expensive and so did his dark-brown gabardine trousers and his French blue shirt and his dark-blue tie that had small brownish-red figures on it that could have been unicorn heads. He wore a pair of gleaming dark-brown alligator ankle boots that must have cost him $150 and maybe even more now that alligators are getting scarce.

Constable's face was wedge-shaped and a curling mass of iron-gray hair grew especially thick along the sides, probably because his big ears stuck out. They had long, thin dangling lobes that were bright pink in color and seemed almost transparent. His eyes were chocolate brown and set deep back underneath heavy brows. His eyes had a damp look about them as if they were always on the verge of tears and I couldn't decide whether that would be a handicap or a help in his profession. His nose was big and fleshy and his mouth, wide and thin-lipped, made him look hungry for some reason. His chin had a deep cleft in it that his female patients must have liked. I didn't much care for it.

"I asked you a question, St. Ives," Constable said.

"I know. You asked me if things are becoming clear."

"Well, are they?"

"It's clear that you intend to kill us. But that shouldn't trouble you much."

"Really? Why?"

"They say that the second time's always easier than the first and that the third time's even easier than the second. I've heard that anyway."

"And you assume that I've already killed somebody?"

"I don't assume it. I know it. You killed a cop called Francis X. Frann."

Constable turned slightly toward Procane, but not enough so that he still didn't have me in full view. "You told me he was really quite quick, didn't you, Abner?"

"All I know is that I told you too much," Procane said.

165

"You liked talking about it. And I liked listening. For a while."

There was a pause that seemed longer than it really was. And then Procane asked his one-word question. The word came out as a choking sound that was filled with disillusionment and shock and even bitterness. Procane asked, "Why?"

Constable didn't answer right away. First he raised himself up on his toes and then let himself back down. He patted his gray hair around the left ear. When he was sure that it was in place he gave his chin a contemplative stroke or two. He seemed to like to touch himself. It may have helped him think.

"Why do you think I killed a young cop, St. Ives? Frann, you called him?"

I was eager to talk. I would have talked all night if he would have listened. I would have told him tales of high adventure and tragic love. If he were still interested, I would have told him about my childhood in Columbus, Ohio, and about how my parents thought I'd caught polio in the summer of 1942 and how they believed that I'd been cured by a Christian Science practitioner that my great-aunt had called in until they discovered that what I had really had was a bad case of the summer flu that was going around that year.

It was the third time that night that a gun had been pointed at me. And this time there was no Janet Whistler or Miles Wiedstein to come out shooting. There was only me, Procane, looking suddenly older and somehow defeated, and a psychoanalyst with a gun who, before he killed me, wanted to know why I thought that he had killed a cop called Francis X. Frann. I decided to tell him. At length, if possible.

"Nobody else could have known about him," I said, my voice cracking just a little on "known." I don't think anyone noticed.

Constable shook his head. He looked disappointed, as if he had been expecting brilliance, but had been met with numskullery. "That isn't sufficient reason," he said.

"Not by itself. But everyone else was accounted for. Janet was with me. Wiedstein was with his wife. Two cops who might have killed him couldn't have. That left either you or Procane. Procane said he didn't kill him so it has to be you."

"Why me?" Constable said. "Why not Procane here despite his denial? Don't you think he's capable of it?"

"That doesn't really enter into it. I guess anyone's capable of murder if sufficiently provoked. Or sufficiently greedy. You were having dinner with Procane that night. He must have already told you about Frann and what he was up to earlier that day. Probably over the phone."

"I told him," Procane said, his voice dulled and flat.

"All right. He told you about Frann. When I came out of my hotel at eight last night, Frann was dead, stabbed to death, sitting in his car in a no-parking zone. He couldn't have been there much more than thirty minutes or the beat cop would have noticed him." I turned my head slowly to look at Procane. "What time did your pal here show up for dinner?"

"Around eight."

"And when did you tell him about Fran?"

"Just after you called me yesterday. Around two, I think."

I looked at Constable. "That gave you nearly six hours to set it up. First you had to locate Frann, arrange a meeting with him, kill him, and then drive him around and park him in front of my hotel. That was a nice touch."

"I thought it would confuse things," Constable said, smiling a little. His teeth were almost the same shade of gray as his hair. I remember wondering whether he had grown up in some section of the country where there was a lot of fluoride in the water supply.

Procane stared at Constable and asked his one-word

question again, "Why?" and once more the word was filled with the melancholy echoes from a shattered faith.

There was a lot of contempt in the look that Constable gave Procane. "Because he could have ruined everything," he said. "You'd have abandoned the entire scheme if Frann had even breathed on you hard. I know you, Abner. Oh, God, how I know you! I had to make sure that Frann was dead and that you knew he was."

"He doesn't mean that," I said.

"Mean what?"

"He doesn't much care about why you killed Frann."

"Oh," Constable said. "I see."

"Well?" I said. "Aren't you going to tell him?"

"We've talked too much already."

"You mind if I tell him?"

"I don't know that you'll have the time."

"It won't take long."

Constable seemed to think about it for a moment before he said, "All right. Tell him."

"A million dollars," I said to Procane and then turned back to Constable. "See. It didn't take long."

My analysis of why he had double-crossed his patient seemed to disappoint Constable. He frowned and gave his head a small, stern shake. "That wasn't it. The money is only the icing."

"All right. You tell him. You owe him that much."

"I don't owe him anything."

"I think you do," Procane said in a low voice. "You owe me that much."

The contempt in Constable's voice matched that in his eyes. "How long have we known each other, Abner, five—six years?"

"About that."

"And all this time you've been talking almost endlessly about how perfectly content you are to be a thief. How perfectly marvelous you think that your chosen career is. You spent hours with me poking at it and probing it and picking away at all the reasons that you think make being a thief the most wonderful thing in the world. And then once a year, or possibly twice, you'd go out and steal more money than I made in a year and then come back and tell me about how easy it was and ask me why more people of intelligence didn't turn to it. Believe it or not, Abner, I'm human. And so when you told me about this million dollars you planned to steal, I became extremely human. I asked myself the old, old question, 'Why him and not me?' And I really didn't come up with any satisfactory answer because, to be quite frank now that I can afford it, I've never really liked you, Abner. I don't like you at all."

To prove it, he shot Procane twice. Procane said something that sounded like "Uff" before he staggered back a step. I didn't watch him fall because I was in the air, throwing myself at Constable's spindly, birdlike legs. My left shoulder caught Constable at the knees and he started to say something like, "No, you don't," but all he could get out was "No, you—" before he went over backward. I heard his gun skitter across part of the oak floor that wasn't covered by the worn oriental rug.

I looked up and saw Constable crawling rapidly after the gun which had skidded almost into the dining room. He would reach it in a few seconds. I turned on my hands and knees and scrambled toward Procane. He looked dead. His mouth was open and so were his eyes. I thought they looked a little crossed.

I reached inside his jacket pocket and felt around until I found the Walther. I jerked it out and when I did I saw that my hand was covered with blood. I turned, still on my knees, and pointed the Walther at Constable. He was turning fast, nearly all the way around now, the .38 revolver in his right hand.

"Hold it right there," I yelled, even then a little self-conscious about the phrase that I had heard a hundred times on television and only once or twice in real life.

He saw my gun and paused, just long enough for me to say, "I can make three holes in your shirt before you can get off your first shot." It was a bluff, of course, and a terribly corny one at that. But I didn't have time to polish it up. All I could do was lock my eyes on his and force a confident smile on my face, the kind that I use when I'm betting a pair of queens into three sixes

I think he almost folded. I'm sure he started to. The muzzle of the gun dipped a little, but then it came back up. He gave his head a small shake, the kind that I've seen poker players give me when they've decided that they'd rather lose their money than suffer the embarrassment of being bluffed.

There wasn't anything else for me to do except pull the trigger. And I did that only because it was better than doing nothing. All I expected to hear was that dry admonishing click of misfire, like the one Procane got when he had tried to shoot the thing at the drive-in. I wasn't really aiming the Walther, just pointing it, so the sound of the blast that it made surprised me.

The large red hole that blossomed where Constable's upper lip had been surprised me even more.

24

Constable was still on his knees and he stayed on them for nearly a second before he slumped forward into a sprawl. The Walther should have knocked him backward, but it hadn't. His damp brown eyes were open and they seemed to be staring at Procane. The lower half of his face was covered with blood and some of it had dripped off and was soaking into the worn oriental rug.

I looked at him for several seconds and then I looked at Procane. After that I looked down at the Walther in my hand. It was smeared with blood, Procane's blood. He would have repaired it, of course. He was like that. Malfunctions probably offended him. On our way back to Washington he would have fixed whatever had gone wrong with the gun. He might have been working on it while Wiedstein was playing chicken with the Oldsmobile.

I remembered that there was a half-bath in the reception hall. I went in there and took a strip of toilet paper and started smearing the blood on the automatic. I flushed the paper down the toilet but kept a small piece wrapped around the trigger guard. I stuck my small finger through the trigger guard and carried the thing that way.

On my way out of the bathroom I caught a glimpse of somebody in the mirror. There was something wrong with his eyes. They glowed a little wild. Something was wrong with his mouth, too. It was half-open and the lips looked loose and slack and almost gray. It looked like the face of someone who wanted to throw up. I clamped my lips together and narrowed my eyes, but it didn't do any good. I still wanted to throw up.

I went back into the living room and stood next to Procane, looking down at him, trying to remember whether he was right- or left-handed. I couldn't remember so I took a chance and carefully placed the automatic near his right hand. Then I knelt, picked up the hand, and inserted it beneath his jacket. I moved it around a little and when I brought it back out it was bloody. I gently placed it on the carpet next to the blood-smeared automatic.

If he were right-handed, they would find traces of

nitrate on it—the result of his bad marksmanship at the drive-in. As for fingerprints, the gun was so smeared with blood that I didn't think they'd worry about them too much. They'd find his prints on its magazine, if they bothered to look.

I moved back to admire my handiwork. It wasn't particularly original, but the newspapers would have a good time with the story. Shoot-outs in Georgetown aren't all that common. The cops would love it, too.

I looked at the three suitcases. I had got them mixed up and couldn't decide which contained the heroin and which contained the money. I picked one at random and tried to open it. It was locked. I took out a nail clipper and started fiddling with the locks. They were cheap cases and the locks proved to be no problem. A sixteen-year-old dropout from Harlem had once spent an afternoon showing me how to pick simple locks. At one time I could open any General Motors car with nothing more than a fingernail file.

I opened the lid of the case. There wasn't any heroin. Just money. They were fifty- and one-hundred-dollar bills, old ones. They were bundled into neat stacks that were bound with strips of brown paper. The figure ten thousand had been written on each strip with a ball-point pen.

The money fascinated me. I must have looked at it for a long time. I thought about how easy it would be to lift out four or five stacks and tuck them away. The inside breast pocket of my jacket would hold two easily. I could get another couple of packets into my hip pockets. They wouldn't be uncomfortable. I heard something and it almost startled me. But it was nothing to worry about. It was only a sigh, a sad one tinged with regret, my own brand.

I closed that suitcase and picked up one of the cases I hadn't opened and took it back to the kitchen. Then I went back and got the remaining one that I hadn't inspected.

I opened them both on the kitchen floor next to the

172

sink. Inside they were packed with carefully arranged double clear-plastic bags. Inside the bags was a white crystalline powder. I picked up one of the bags. It seemed to weigh a little more than a pound. I turned on the water in the sink and then ripped the bag open. I wet my finger and stuck it inside the plastic bag and then gave my finger a tentative tongue lick. It wasn't milk sugar.

I found the switch for the disposal and turned it on. It made a harsh, grinding roar. I dumped the white powder into the sink. The water caught it and swirled it down the drain. It took me nearly thirty minutes to open the hundred half-kilo plastic bags and flush a million dollars' worth of heroin down the disposal and into the sewer system that led to the Potomac. I found myself wondering what it would do to the fish and decided that that was something else for the Izaak Walton League to worry about.

I gathered up the empty plastic bags and put them into one of the suitcases. I found a sponge and carefully mopped up the drainboard, the sink, and the floor. I let the disposal and the water run for another five minutes. It they took the plumbing apart, they could probably find traces of heroin. If they were looking for it. I didn't think that they would be.

I carried the suitcases back into the living room. The one that contained the empty plastic bags I carried into the half-bath in the reception hall. I took the bags out five at a time and flushed them down the toilet. There were a hundred of them and I had to flush the toilet twenty times. I would have used the living room fireplace, but fire doesn't do much to plastic except melt it into a smelly glob. I don't know what fire does to heroin. Probably nothing.

After I was finished in the bathroom, I picked up the two empty suitcases and started up the stairs. The fourth floor was an attic. I thought it would be. Old houses like that have attics. This one was full of junk. There was a bureau with peeling veneer. A couple of old-fashioned steamer trunks. Some heavy cardboard boxes with twine tied around them. Three rolled-up rugs. A forty-year-old RCA radio-phonograph, as big as a small pony, with cabinet work that was too good to throw away. Five four-foot stacks of the *National Geographic*. Three shadeless floor lamps, and a dusty couch covered with velveteen that had worn spots on its arms and back.

The couch was against the wall so I pulled it out enough to put the two suitcases behind it. I piled some copies of the *National Geographic* on top of the cases. They might be found tomorrow or next year. I didn't really care.

I went back downstairs and looked around the living room. My watch said it was eleven-fifteen. I lit a cigarette and looked about for something else that I could tidy up. I didn't see anything except the two dead bodies, but there was nothing else that I could do for them.

I used the toilet to get rid of the cigarette. Then I went back and picked up the suitcase that held the million dollars. It weighed about thirty pounds. That's what a million dollars should have weighed at 490 bills to the pound. Ten thousand fifty-dollar bills. Five thousand one-hundred-dollar bills. Thirty pounds of money. A million dollars.

Carrying the suitcase, I went carefully down the back stairs into the garden. I followed the glittering white path to the alley where I stopped to rest. My arm ached. I picked up the suitcase again and made it to the end of the alley where I put it down again. Thirty pounds shouldn't have been that heavy, but by the time that I got to Wisconsin Avenue I had put it down and picked it up ten times.

There weren't any cabs, of course. I stood at the curb, the suitcase at my feet, and waved at anything that went by. A young kid of about twenty with long hair and a Chester A. Arthur moustache watched me for a while. He was leaning against a wall, wrapped up in an old army officer's overcoat that was three sizes too big for him. When he got tired of watching me he came over and said, "Excuse me, sir, have you got any spare change?"

I found forty-two cents in my pants pocket and handed it to him. I always do. They're the future of the country. "Have a good time," I said.

He looked at the coins. "Thank you, sir. Now I can buy a gallon of gas."

"Have you got a car?"

"Well, it's sort of a car."

"It's worth ten bucks for me to get to National Airport."

At the mention of ten dollars his eyes lit up. As I said, they're the future of our country. "You're almost there," he said. "I'll be right back."

He was right. It was sort of a car. Fifteen years ago or so it had been used to deliver milk. Now it was covered with various shades of glo-paint and a lot of bright sayings such as, "Free Sirhan Sirhan" and "Save our Piranhas."

The kid helped me store the suitcase in the back where the milk used to be. Now it contained a mattress, a small gasoline stove, a frying pan, and a cardboard box of canned goods. "Home," the kid said.

"Looks lived in," I said and went around to the front of the truck. At one time there had been a folding seat behind the wheel for the milkman to sit on. But it was gone and the kid had to drive standing up all the way to National Airport. I couldn't feel sorry for him because there was nothing for me to sit on either.

"You a salesman?" he asked when we were almost there.

"Yes," I said.

"It figures."

"Why?"

"That suitcase. It was heavy."

"I know."

It was eleven forty-five by the time we got to Eastern's entrance at the airport. I gave the kid his ten dollars and he thanked me and we went back and got the case out of the rear.

"I'd help you with it but I can't double park here."

"That's okay."

He eyed the suitcase. He wanted something else so I waited to find out what it was. Finally he said, "Why dontcha let me have a free sample?"

I shook my head. "You wouldn't like it."

"Why?"

"It makes some people sick."

That interested him. Drugs would. "How sick?"

"Some people die from it," I said, picked up the case, and walked toward the terminal.

I managed to buy a seat on a midnight flight to New York. After I checked the suitcase through I found a pay phone, dropped in a dime, and dialed 444-1111. When the man's voice said, "Police Emergency, Officer Welch," I said, "There're two men dead." Then I slowly recited the number on N Street.

"Northeast?" he said.

"No," I said. "Northwest. In Georgetown."

25

Miles Wiedstein and Janet Whistler listened in silence until I had finished telling them about Procane and Constable and what I had done with the heroin.

They were seated in a couple of chairs in my apartment. I was at the poker table. The suitcase rested on top of it. It was closed.

A silence began when I stopped talking. It continued for several moments. Finally, Wiedstein said, "I want to drink."

"That's't dumb," Janet Whistler said.

"I didn't say I was going to have one; I said I wanted one."

"There's some Scotch and gin over there," I said, nodding toward the Pullman kitchen.

"Don't force it on him."

"It's there if he wants it."

"I don't want it enough," Wiedstein said. "Not yet."

"The cops will know we were there," Janet Whistler said. "Mrs. Williams will tell them we were there."

"We had dinner with Procane," I said. "That's all. Then we left. At eight-twenty."

"And drove around," Wiedstein said. "Sightseeing."

I nodded. "That's right."

"What if the neighbors were snoopy?" Janet said.

"It doesn't matter," Wiedstein said. "If they were, they saw the four of us come back. Two men went in the house. It could have been Procane and Constable —not Procane and St. Ives."

"I wandered around on my own after dinner." I said. "I caught a picture I'd missed in New York. Then I flew back here."

Janet Whistler looked at Wiedstein once more. "What was Constable doing with us?"

"Visiting Procane," he said. "We picked him up at the airport after we let St. Ives out downtown."

We sat there for several moments, thinking about our alibis and how rotten they were. But unless the police got lucky, we would never have to prove them. And if the police got really lucky, alibis wouldn't matter in the least.

Wiedstein rose, walked over to the kitchen, and took down a bottle of Scotch. He uncorked it and sniffed the aroma. He put the cork back and replaced the bottle. He turned and looked at Janet for a moment. Then he looked at me.

"What do you think your cut should be, St. Ives?"

"Of a million dollars?"

"That's right. Of a million dollars."

"Nothing."

He let himself look surprised. "Scruples?" he said. "It's a little late for those, isn't it?"

"I'm all out of scruples," I said.

"What about a third?" he said. "You killed Constable. That should be worth about a third of a million."

"To you?" I said.

He nodded. "Sure. To me. Why not?"

I shook my head. "No thanks."

He turned to Janet Whistler. "Well?"

"Well what?"

"How do you want to split it?"

"I don't care," she said. "I'm not going to fight over it. If we start fighting over it, one of us will wind up dead. It's not worth that. Not to me anyway. Do what you want to with it."

"You want me to tell you how much you get?"

"Yes, she said, "that would be all right."

"A fourth," Wiedstein said.

"A fourth," she said. "Fine. A quarter of a million. Two-hundred-and-fifty-thousand. That's fine."

"Count it out," he said.

She rose and moved toward the poker table. She walked slowly. When she was halfway there she turned toward me and made a small, somehow helpless gesture. "Have you got anything I could put it in?"

"I'll find something," I said.

She nodded and continued toward the poker table. When she reached it she turned and looked back at Wiedstein. "You're taking the rest?"

"Would you object?"

She shook her head. "No, I wouldn't object."

I went to a closet and rummaged through it until I

found a ziparound overnight bag. I carried it over to the poker table. "Here," I said. "You can use this."

She zipped open the bag and then lifted the top of the suitcase. For nearly a minute she stood there and stared at the money. Wiedstein rose and moved over to the table and also stared at it. I stared, too.

"Count it out," Wiedstein told her.

She nodded and started placing ten-thousand-dollar packets in the overnight bag. The ones made up of hundred-dollar bills were approximately half an inch high. The ones with fifty-dollar bills were twice that. After she put twenty-four of the packets in the overnight bag, she took a ten-thousand-dollar packet of fifty-dollar bills, stripped off its paper band, carelessly divided it, and placed about half of the bills in her purse, the rest in the overnight case.

"That's it," she said, zipping up the case.

"Not quite," Wiedstein said.

"What else?" she said.

"Insurance." He started counting ten-thousand-dollar packets onto the poker table. When he had counted fifty of them onto the table, he closed the suitcase and looked to me.

"Now you're in just as deep, St. Ives."

"A half-million dollars' worth," I said.

"Procane's share," Wiedstein said and picked up the suitcase that now contained his own share—a quarter of a million. "Come on," he said to Janet, "I'll give you a ride home."

"I don't want it," I said.

"You've got it anyway."

They moved toward the door, each of them carrying a small fortune and leaving a larger one behind. Wiedstein opened the door. Janet Whistler gave me a small wave of her hand and then went through it. She didn't say good-bye. She just waved.

"What'll I do with it?" I said.

Wiedstein stopped at the open door and looked at

me, a small smile on his face. "With half a million dollars?" he said.

"Yes."

"You'll think of something."

26

Myron Greene had a big desk but a half-million dollars managed to make it look small.

"Is it all there?" I said.

Greene looked up. He was counting the money. For the third time. "It's what you said it was. Five hundred thousand."

"Well?"

He shook his head and frowned. "It's stolen money."

"It doesn't look stolen."

"I mean there's no source for it. No legitimate one at any rate."

"Make it an anonymous contribution."

He shook his head again. "Did you ever hear of anyone who gave away half a million dollars anonymously?"

"The most I every gave anonymously was five dollars," I said. "After that I wanted credit."

"The IRS would—well, I don't even want to think about it."

"We can split it."

He looked up at me. "You're kidding, of course?"

"Not necessarily. If you can't think of a method to

give it away, we can keep it. You can invest my share for me."

"But it's Procane's money."

"Procane's dead and it wasn't his money. It belonged to the drug dealers. He stole it from them and I helped. They got it from the junkies. Procane wanted to give it to that drug clinic up in Harlem. He seemed to enjoy the irony of the idea. But you say it can't be done."

Myron Green frowned again. "I didn't say it couldn't be done. I said it would be difficult."

I got up and moved toward the door. "Let me know how you work it out."

"Wait a minute."

"What?"

He walked around his desk, picked up a packet of the money, and riffled through it. He looked at the money and then at me.

"You could have kept it all, couldn't you?"

"Yes."

"And there would have been no way to trace it?"

"None. Almost none anyway."

"And you helped steal it?"

I shrugged. "I suppose I helped. At least I didn't get in the way."

"But you can't keep it."

"No, I can't keep it."

"I want to ask why."

"Go ahead."

"All right, why can't you keep it?"

I had to give him some sort of an answer. It wasn't going to be completely true, but Myron Greene was far too experienced a lawyer to expect the complete truth from anyone.

"You're not going to believe me," I said.

He nodded. "I know."

"But you want to hear it anyway."

"That's right."

"By not keeping the money I may be trying to prove something."

"What?"

"Something that I don't believe exists."

"I'll ask what again."

"A good thief."

Myron Greene thought that over for a moment. "And have you? Proved it, I mean."

"I don't know."

"Yes," he said, "I can see how you wouldn't."